Pre-Revelation

Pre-Revelation

Travis J. Payne

Copyright © 2011 by Travis J. Payne.

Library of Congress Control Number: 2010917864
ISBN: Hardcover   978-1-4568-2639-0
          Softcover   978-1-4568-2638-3
          Ebook   978-1-4568-2640-6

All rights reserved. No part of this book may be reproduced or transmitted in any form or by any means, electronic or mechanical, including photocopying, recording, or by any information storage and retrieval system, without permission in writing from the copyright owner.

This is a work of fiction. Names, characters, places and incidents either are the product of the author's imagination or are used fictitiously, and any resemblance to any actual persons, living or dead, events, or locales is entirely coincidental.

This book was printed in the United States of America.

To order additional copies of this book, contact:
Xlibris Corporation
1-888-795-4274
www.Xlibris.com
Orders@Xlibris.com
90912

Chapter 1

The night sky is ravaged by thunder; the clouds are dark and overshadow the landscape like a blanket. The thunder is louder with each crushing sound penetrating the air. Lightning appears in the clouds, turning their dark complexion into rays of white. Rain falls, hitting the ground, sounding like tiny beads falling from a table. The clouds begin to converge, the lightning strikes ground. There's an explosion, the lightning stops but rain continues. There is a hole in the ground that was a result of the lightning, in it, crouched down with wings the color of red wrapped around him, is an angel. Not just any angel—an archangel, and his name is Zerach. With no mercy, he punishes those who have sinned; all the while, he is an angel of justice, kind and heroic. An extrovert who will sacrifice his life to save those worthy of the Lord's grace. As he rises from the giant hole in the ground created from the thunder, his wings retract into his back. Zerach is dressed in angelic battle armor, which covers his neck, torso, legs, and feet. His chest armor is made from silver; on it is a piece of scripture written in the angelic language. It translates to angel of fire, written across it. His eyes are bright, shining like silver coins. Zerach walked onto a road; there wasn't a car in miles. He figured it would be best to follow the road and see where it took him. Zerach needed to find someplace to change clothes; his armor really stood out, and he needed to blend in with the humans. Zerach walked until he entered a freeway on ramp; the cars were coming fast, not paying him any attention. As calm as a breeze, Zerach stepped on the highway. The cars swerved around him, honking their horns at him, one driver yelled at him. He finally made his way down a hill which led to a small plaza. There were a number of businesses, such as restaurants and a grocery store. The plaza faced a busy street, which seemed to never sleep. Cars were speeding up and down the road. Zerach made his way to a Macy's. It looked as if it had been in the plaza for a long time. Zerach walked in still dressed in his armor. He was approached by an employee. He was a young man in his late teens, dressed in bright blue jeans and a worn-out yellow shirt. He had on a pair of glasses with brown rims; he was reading *People* magazine. Zerach caught his attention, and he looked up and was startled by him. "Sir, the store is closed," he said, stopping Zerach from entering. Zerach looked at him, touching his chest with his pointer finger. "Shhh," that was all he had to say as the employee fainted and dropped to the floor. Zerach made his way to the men's department. He looked around looking for something suitable to wear. He found some T-shirts folded on a shelf; they were in a variety of colors, but Zerach decided to wear a white button-down shirt. Zerach picked out some dark jeans and a pair of black Converse tennis shoes. Zerach gathered what he had and entered a dressing room. He put the clothes on; he removed his armor. His dark skin glistening in the mirror was a sight to see. Attached to his back was a strap that contained two swords. Zerach pushed a button on each handle, turning them into small sticks and then placed them in his pocket. As Zerach was walking out, he caught a glimpse of a black trench coat hanging on a rack. Zerach took it off the rack and put it on. He looked at himself in the mirror and was impressed; he walked out of the store, now ready to fulfill his mission to secure the most divine entity—the Holy Grail. The Holy Grail is not an object; it is a person, a living, breathing human being. Her life will determine the fate of mankind, for she holds the key to humanity's fate.

Chapter 2

As Zerach arrived on earth, another arrives with an interest in the Holy Grail, with the purpose of becoming God and taking over hell. He was not interested in protecting her, his interest lied within her soul. For it could grant him the power to become a god and rule hell. His name is Jaricus, vicious and tenacious, who had the power to devour souls; each one made him stronger. The earth shook with rage, the ground cracked. Like an open wound, black liquid seeped through the cracks, and Jaricus rose from the ground in an empty parking lot. He climbed out of the hole, crawling on his stomach; his clothes were torn and mangled, and steam came out from his skin. He was in the middle of an empty parking lot. He looked around and saw a store that read "Hot Topic." Jaricus approached the store, breaking down the door. The alarm system turned on, but Jaricus didn't care; he picked out a trench coat, a shirt, and black pants. Jaricus then slipped on some boots, his long jet black hair stretched down to his shoulders. Hare eyes red as roses glow in the dark. The police arrived and confronted him at the entrance of the store. "Sir, I'm sorry, but you can't be here. You're trespassing," said the officer. Jaricus stared at him with unblinking eyes. "Sir, did you hear what I just said?" Jaricus tilted his head to the left, then to the right. "Yes, yes, I heard you just fine, but I'm afraid you are wasting my time."

"Sir, I'm not going to tell you again. Either you leave willingly or I'm going to have to take you in. What's it going to be?" Jaricus looked at the ground and then at the sky, then back at the officer. "I choose to take your car." The officer drew his gun and, in an assertive manner, yelled, "Put your hands on your head!" Jaricus raised his hands over his head. "Now walk over to me slow!" Jaricus walked over to the officer who still had his gun pointed right at his face. Jaricus stood at the hood of the cop car. "Now put your hand behind your back." As the officer reached for Jaricus's hand, Jaricus ripped the officer's arm off. The cop yelled in agony, and then Jaricus snapped the officer's neck. He got into the car, turned on the radio, gone through channels, seeking any suitable music he may find amusing. Jaricus finally found a music channel; they were playing heavy metal, something Jaricus took a liking to. He turned on the car and sped out of the parking lot down the street.

Alexa, who just turned eighteen, lives the life of any privileged teenager. Her family is rich, perhaps the wealthiest family in Newport. She is a down-to-earth girl who is captain of the cheerleading team. She has brown hair with light brown eyes and a smile that can make a man freeze. Her hair came down to her shoulders; it was wavy and beautiful. It was her second semester, and spring break was approaching. She was anticipating going out and partying, but little did she know, fate would bring about a change of plans. Alexa was in the girls' locker room, taking a shower. The water was running down her body, the soap slowly dripping downward like honey. As Alexa reached for the shampoo, something caught her eye. "Who's there?" she called out. Startled, Alexa turned off the water and went to the dressing room. Shrieking, clawing noises rattled the room as if someone had taken some sharp nails, scratching lockers.

"Whoever it is, stop it!" Alexa shrieked; out of the shadows came her best friend Jennifer. "Alexa, what are you doing?"

"Was that you who were making that noise?"

"Yeah, I didn't mean to scare you. Listen, you going to that party this Saturday?" asked Jennifer. Alexa leaned back against a locker. "Yeah, but Chris is going to be there."

"C'mon," Jennifer pleaded. "It'll be fun. Don't let Chris ruin your spring break." Alexa had been with a guy named Chris on and off for two years. She was getting tired of all his crap and just wanted to have fun this spring break. "I don't know. He's been such an asshole! I mean, he goes out with his friends doing God knows what, and when I go out, he always accuses me of hooking up with another guy," said Alexa

"Who did he accuse you of hooking up with?" asked Jennifer.

"Daniel! Of all people."

"Oh my god! You serious?" asked Jennifer, baffled by what Alexa told her. Alexa sat down on the bench. "Yes, Daniel of all people. He and I are friends, but c'mon, he already has a girlfriend." Alexa put her shoes on and grabbed her backpack. She and Jennifer walked down a hallway when they came across Chris and his friend Michael, who were talking among themselves. "You going to that party on Saturday?" asked Chris. "Yeah, I don't have anything else to do," replied Michael. Chris is tall and muscular. He often wore a red football jacket with his last name across the back, and his black hair was short and cropped. Chris's friend Michael was a bro. He drove a black raised truck that can be heard a block away because he was always blasting loud music. "What do you say we stop by Alexa's house?" asked Chris. Suddenly, he noticed Alexa and Jennifer walking toward him and Michael. "Hey, what's up?" asked Chris, giving Alexa a hug. "Nothing, you?" replied Alexa with a sigh in her voice. "Is everything okay?"

"Everything is fine, just going home." Alexa walked off with Jennifer while Chris and Michael stood in disbelief. "Dude, what was that all about?" asked Michael with a smirk on his face. "How the hell should I know? She's being really bitchy. I don't give a fuck what she does anymore." As Chris and Michael stood in the hallway, a man dressed in a black coat stood at the opposite end of the hall. His eyes glared red; then as quickly as he appeared, he vanished.

Alexa and Jennifer were driving in the car on their way home. They drove up to an In-N-Out burger restaurant where they decided to get something to eat. As they pulled up, they noticed a red sports car parked in front of them. Out came a suspicious young man dressed in a black trench coat and black pants.

"Look at that guy over there," said Alexa, pointing straight ahead.

"Who? The guy sitting on his car? What about him?"

"He's just been sitting there staring at me," Alexa says.

"Well, he's hot!" Jennifer muttered, taking another sip of her soda.

"He's really freaking me out."

"Let's go talk to him," suggested Jennifer.

"Would you sit down!" exclaimed Alexa, nervous by this unknown stranger who would not take his eyes off her. Then the stranger got into his car and drove off down the street. This came at a very confusing moment for Alexa, who never felt so worried in her life. "C'mon, girl, you need to have some fun while you're still young."

"I have a boyfriend, remember?" said Alexa, taking a bite of her burger.

"Yeah, and you don't have a ring on that finger. Besides, we live in SoCal, and summer is coming up. It is the time and place to meet new guys, which I suggest you do," replied Jennifer, eating some of Alexa's fries.

"That guy just really seemed weird to me. Like he could see right through me."

"Maybe he's someone you used to know from back in the day."

"No, I would remember. That guy is a total stranger. Maybe we should go now," Alexa suggested, feeling too uncomfortable to finish her food. She and Jennifer walked back to her car and drove home. Later that night, Alexa was having a nightmare. In her dream, she was lying on a stone cross, her hands and feet were tied down. She had on a black cloak with a white cross painted on it, along with a crown on her head. She was staring upward at the face of an unknown man who was standing over her. It was Jaricus; he was wearing a gold cloak, and knife was in his hands. His eyes glistened, staring into Alexa's eyes. And then, he thrust the knife into Alexa's chest. She jumped outright before it all ended. Alexa was confused, terrified, wondering why she had such a dream.

To her, it seemed so real, as if she were actually there. Alexa looked at the clock, it was four o'clock in the morning, and she needed to get some sleep. Alexa went to bed thinking to herself, reminiscing about the dream. The man she saw earlier that day popped into her head, and she wondered if her dream had something to do with him. Alexa will soon find out.

Chapter 3

The next morning, Alexa got up and took a quick shower before getting ready for school. She got dressed and put her make up on, just looking forward to another day at school. Alexa got into her car and drove to school. On her way, she saw the same guy she had seen earlier before. This time, he pulled up next to her and stared at her; Alexa couldn't help but stare back at him. She had no clue she was looking at Zerach, the angel sent to protect her from Jaricus. Alexa sat there in her car, waiting for the light to turn green. She couldn't take her eyes off him. Zerach kept starring at her as if reading her thoughts, knowing that she was the one he must protect. After sitting in front of a red light, which felt like an eternity, the light turned green. Alexa looked in her rearview mirror, nothing! Zerach had disappeared, and Alexa wondered who this stranger was. She pulled into the student parking lot where Jennifer was waiting for her.

"Alexa, how's it . . . Are you okay?" Jennifer said, realizing Alexa was disturbed about something.

"I saw him."

"You saw who?"

"The guy at In-N-Out, remember? The one who was sitting on his car." Jennifer stood next to Alexa, putting her arm around her. "Maybe it was just a coincidence, you don't think he could be stalking you?" Alexa sat back, reflecting back to her dream. "No, it was him. I seriously think he is following me."

"Alexa, relax, okay? Nothing is going to happen, and besides, he's pretty hot," said Jennifer, laughing.

"No, I'm not joking! He was . . ."

"He was what?" asked Jennifer, brushing her hair back.

"Nothing. He just had this necklace. Anyways, it's probably nothing."

"Now, c'mon, let's think about that party tomorrow. So what are you going to wear?"

As the girls walked away, just a few feet behind, perched on a rooftop, squatting down, Zerach kept his watchful eye on Alexa, waiting for the right time when Jaricus will strike. Zerach said to himself, "I've found you. Now where are you, Jaricus?"

Lunch arrived; Alexa was eating her lunch when Chris walked up by himself. "Hey, what's going on?" asked Chris, sitting next to Alexa. "Nothing. What's going on with you?"

"I've been good, just waiting for school to end." Danny came out of nowhere interrupting Alexa and Chris's conversation. "My girlfriend and I broke up."

"I'm sorry, Danny." Alexa put her arm around Danny, giving him some support. Chris sat there angry as can be. "Alexa, everyone is talking about formal, and I was wondering if you would like to go with me?" Danny asked in a shy voice. Chris couldn't believe what he just heard. "Sorry, Danny, I'm already going with Chris."

"That's cool, maybe next time." Chris stood up, putting his arm around Alexa.

"There won't be a next time," said Chris in a cocky tone. Danny just stood there, pissed off, before walking away, shaking his head.

"What the hell is your problem?"

"What? That kid is an idiot, okay? He's been after you since sophomore year," Chris said, trying to keep up with Alexa. "Look, Chris, you don't control me, okay? Besides, we're not even together, so you better be careful."

"Whatever you say. Listen, I still care about you. I don't see why we can't work it out?" Alexa walked away to her first class of the day without saying a word. During lunch, all the kids were talking about formal, especially the girls. Alexa was eating her lunch with Jennifer gossiping about whatever until something caught Alexa's eye. In the middle of the quad drinking a coke, Zerach was sitting on a bench, watching her.

No one seemed to notice him except Alexa. She was not afraid; in fact, she wanted to talk to him. "Hold on."

"Alexa, where are you going?" Before Jennifer had a chance to finish, Alexa had gotten up. As she approached Zerach, he walked away. "Wait!

Why are you following me?" Alexa yelled, but it was too late. Zerach walked off too fast and disappeared. Alexa didn't know what was going on. Saturday, it was the night of the big house party. People were inside mingling with one another. The house was a mansion about three stories, full of teenagers who came from all over the county. Alexa was inside with Jennifer sitting on a couch. A DJ was playing some music, while people danced or drank. The party was going on well, and everyone was having a great time. What they didn't know was their fun was going to be cut short. Across the street, Jaricus stood motionless, as still as a statue.

Jaricus casually walked across the street. He approached Chris and Mike. They were outside, sitting by the front door, drinking beer. They were with a group of girls. Jaricus approached them as if he knew who they were. "Who's this?"

A girl asked looking at Jaricus with wide eyes. Jaricus stood there looking around, observing the party. "Can I help you? . . . You lost?" Mike stood up, a bottle of beer in his hand. Jaricus looked at him. "I am looking for Alexa. Is she here?" Chris got up. He stepped toward Jaricus, looking at him in his eyes. "How about you turn around an—" Jaricus punched Chris through the chest and ripped his heart out.

"You were saying?" said Jaricus, taking the heart and crushing it with his hand.

The girls screamed and ran inside. They everyone came out to see what was going on. "Oh shit!" exclaimed Mike, trying to run.

"Where do you think you're going?" Jaricus grabbed Mike by the neck and tore his head off. The blood ran down like water. He crushed Mike's head and then licked the blood.

"Time to party," said Jaricus, smiling.

Everyone ran in a panic; Jaricus blew down the door.

"What's going on?" Alexa looked around. "Run!" someone yelled. Jaricus walked through the house; he grabbed a kid by the shirt. "Where's Alexa?"

"I don't know what you're talking about."

"Then you are useless to me." Jaricus placed his hands on the guy's cheeks, turning his body into flames. Jaricus walked through the house, butchering every person he could find. He took one girl and filled her lungs with tar. He kept snatching anyone in his way, dispatching them with his own hands. All in an attempt to find what is rightfully his, the Holy Grail—Alexa.

Jennifer grabbed Alexa. "Let's go!" They ran outside, Jaricus caught Alexa's sent and shot through the ceiling of the roof, landing in front of Alexa and Jennifer. Jaricus very coolly and calmly whispered, "Hello, Alexa."

Chapter 4

Alexa and Jennifer both stood there, fear gripping both of them. Jaricus looked at Jennifer, his eyes unblinking. Jennifer's brain swelled, blood came out of her eyes, nose, mouth, and ears. "Jennifer!" Alexa grabbed her, while blood continued to come out.

"What did you do?" Jaricus grabbed Alexa by her hair, she screamed, trying to get free, but it was no use. Jaricus finally had his prize, and he couldn't wait to get the power he deserved. At times like these, one would assume that the worst is going to happen. That is what went through Alexa's mind. Just when she thought all hope was gone, a savior arrived. Out of nowhere, a sword plunged through Jaricus's chest. Zerach came out of nowhere, pulled the sword out of Jaricus and kicked him in the stomach, sending him through a car. "Come with me!" Zerach reached his hand out to Alexa. She hesitated, not sure if she could trust him or not. "Okay." Alexa took Zerach's hand; they ran off across the street and into a red sports car. They sped off into the night. "Who are you?"

"My name is Zerachiel; I was sent here to protect you, but you can call me Zerach." Zerach made a sharp turn onto a highway.

"Who sent you?"

"God." Zerach was focused on the road. Alexa didn't know what to think. She thought she was going crazy.

"So who are you?" Zerach pulled over; he looked Alexa in the eyes.

"Calm down. My name is Zerach; I was sent here by God. His orders are to protect you at all costs."

"What? From who?" asked Alexa, shaking so much that her seat shook.

"Jaricus. That man back there that attacked that party, his name is Jaricus. He wants you."

"Why? For what?"

"To take your soul and use it to become a god." Zerach sat back in his seat, started the car, and drove to a gas station down the street. Alexa sat in the car, her mind racing, thinking about tonight. Zerach parked the car and then went inside to pay for the gas. Alexa thought it was her chance, her chance to escape. Alexa slipped out of the car as quietly as she could. She ran in the opposite direction of the car, and then Zerach was in front of her in the blink of an eye. Zerach grabbed her by the arm. Alexa screamed. "Let me go! I don't want any part of this!"

"You don't have a choice," Zerach said calmly. "You will do exactly as I tell you; do as I say when I say so." Zerach took Alexa back to the car. She sat in the passenger seat, trying to relax. Alexa thought to herself, What's going on? What have I done wrong? Can he help me? Who is he? Alexa didn't know what to do or think. Zerach sat in the front seat. He looked at Alexa and asked, "Do you trust me?"

Alexa didn't know how to answer the question. How was she supposed to know if this guy wasn't going to kill her? "Yes, I trust you."

"Good, we need to get—" Jaricus grabbed Zerach through the windshield of the car, throwing him to the pavement. "You motherfucker!" Jaricus grabbed Zerach by the collar. Zerach headbutted Jaricus in the face, and then kicked him in the stomach. Jaricus went through the window of the store, where cashier worked. "Alexa, get in the car." Alexa did as she was told.

Zerach got in on the driver's side, and Jaricus ran after them with lightning speed. He grabbed the back bumper of the car.

"Hold on." Zerach told Alexa, holding her in his arms, jumping out of the vehicle. Jaricus grabbed Zerach and took the car and tore the back end apart. Zerach clenched his fists. "You won't have her!" yelled Zerach, knocking Jaricus to the ground. Jaricus threw him in the air. Zerach came crashing down on top of a black pick-up truck.

"I can have her now," said Jaricus, turning his attention on Alexa. "Well, pretty girl, you're all mine." Jaricus raised his hand; Alexa's body went numb. She couldn't feel her arms or legs. Her body was frozen stiff and started to glide across the ground toward Jaricus. Zerach teleported in front of Jaricus and dug his hands into his stomach and then threw him into the window of the gas station. Zerach and Alexa took off in the car.

Back at the house party, dead bodies lay everywhere. Police, forensics, and paramedics were on the property. It was a gruesome site; blood stained the walls. Chunks of flesh splattered on the counter tops. Two cops walked in, their names are Tom and Captain Jason. Jason is a veteran on the force. He is tall, with brown hair and a brown mustache.

He was dressed in a brown jacket with a black tie. His hair was slick back; a pair of glasses rested on his face. His partner Tom was young, ambitious, and hot headed. His black jacket was leather; looking like something a biker would wear. Tom didn't dress the way a typical detective dressed. First of all, he wore dark blue jeans. Tom had Converse tennis shoes on his feet as well. "Jason, you've seen anything like this?"

"How bad is it?" said Jason, stepping behind Tom.

"This is nothing I've ever seen before. It's a fucking massacre," Tom said, taking a piece of cloth from a dead body. "They were ripped to shreds like cattle." Jason kneeled next to Tom. "How many alive?"

"There's only ten witnesses; all the others are dead," replied Tom, scoping the living room for any more clues. "It appears this guy enjoyed ripping their heads off and gouging out their eyes. Along with their hearts," said Tom, shining a light on the bodies. Since Tom was fairly new, he had never seen anything like this before. Jason walked outside to speak to a witness. A girl in her early teens was outside, shaken up. All she could do was stare at the ground. "I got it from here," Jason told a paramedic who was stitching the girls arm. "My name is Detective Jason; I need to ask you some questions. Is that okay?" Jason showed the girl his badge and let her look at as he placed it in her hand. The girl nodded. "Good. This will only take a minute, I promise." Jason sat beside her, as if he were her best friend.

"Tell me, what did you see?" he asked in almost a whisper. The girl looked at him in his eyes then put her head down. "It all happened so fast," she said, tears coming down her face.

"It's okay, everything's going to be fine. You can trust me. Tell me, what's your name?"

"My name is Maria." Jason put his arm around her. "Well, Maria, you have absolutely nothing to worry about. I'm here for you. Okay?" said Jason, smiling at Maria. "Now, can you think real hard to what happened tonight?" Maria straightened up a bit, pressed her shoulders back. "He came into the living room. At first I thought he was there for the party. Out of nowhere, he just started killing people."

"That's it?" asked Jason. Maria turned her head away. Jason stood up. "All right then, if you have—"

"He was after someone," Maria mumbled under her breath.

"He was looking for whom?" asked Jason.

"He was looking for a girl that goes to my school"

"What's her name?" asked Jason, taking out a pen and notepad. Maria looked at him with stern eyes. "Her name is Alexa. She's captain of the cheerleading team."

Jason leaned next to Maria. "You did the right thing; everything's going to be fine."

Tom approached Jason with a startled look on his face. "Jason, I found something." Jason followed Tom to the back of the house. On the wall was a burned imprint of a cross. The cross was white, with a red jewel in the middle of it. "Take it down, for evidence," Jason said, examining it closely.

Tom and Jason got back in their car, heading straight back to the precinct. "What the hell was that?" asked Tom, concentrating on the road, while Jason was sitting in the passenger seat, analyzing the scene. "It looked like some Satan shit."

"Whatever or whoever it was, is still out there. Had to be at least five guys."

"No, it was one."

"How do you know?" asked Tom, with suspicion in his tone.

"I know because I spoke to a witness. Something you have yet to learn, kid."

They pulled up to the precinct and were greeted by a forensic scientist, Jack Little. He was a tall, slim man. He was wearing a white lab coat and beige pants. "While performing an autopsy on the victims, I discovered some sort of unknown markings on all of them."

"What markings?" asked Tom.

"If you look closely, all the victims have a rare carving into their chests. It is as if the person responsible was a member of a cult."

Meanwhile, Zerach and Alexa settled in a hotel. Alexa sat on the bed, not sure whether Zerach was crazy or telling the truth. She lay back on the bed, thinking to herself. Alexa thought about how she got into all this mess. Zerach sat outside, on the edge of the balcony. Alexa found the courage to get up and go talk to him, seeing if she could get any answers. "So who is this Jaricus guy?"

"He's a demon," Zerach said, looking at the sky.

"All right, well, what does he want?"

"He wants you," replied Zerach, still staring off into the sky. Alexa didn't know what to think of this and decided to ask another question. "Why does he want me?"

Zerach turned to look at her. "He wants your soul to become a god."

"And I'll act like this never happened," said Alexa desperate to leave.

"You don't understand. I can't allow that Jaricus will find you. You're better off staying here."

"But—" Zerach cut her off, his eyes turning silver.

"But nothing. If you go home, that will be the first place he will look. Besides, your parents are dead. Jaricus most likely killed them already." Alexa pushed Zerach and started crying. "You don't know that!" Zerach grabbed Alexa by the arms, slamming her on the bed. "Look at me. Look at me!"

Zerach lay on top of Alexa, pinning her to the bed, resting his eyes on hers. "Get this through your head: you are in this whether you like it or not. There's no going back. Jaricus will not stop until he has what he wants. You are the key to mankind's salvation, and for that, I can never let you leave." Alexa got up abruptly, darting to the door. Zerach appeared in front of her in a flash.

"Please don't hurt me just let me go."

"I can't allow that Alexa. Your life is in great danger. You are better off sticking with me. If you go out there, you will fall into the wrong hands."

Alexa sat down quietly on the bed; she curled up in a ball, staring at Zerach, who sat next to her.

Zerach whispered to her very softly saying, "Everything will be okay. I promise I won't let anything bad happen to you."

Alexa turned to look at Zerach in his eyes; her legs were stretched out, her head resting on the pillow. "How do I know I can trust you?" asked Alexa with twinkling eyes, as if she was looking into the eyes of the man of her dreams.

"All I give you is my word and my life," said Zerach, wiping the tears from Alexa's face that looked at Zerach.

"I trust you."

Zerach lay next to her, staring at her. Alexa was fast asleep. All Zerach could think about was Alexa. He had never seen a human so beautiful in his life. He wanted nothing more but to be by her side, and he would die to protect her.

The next morning, there was a knock at the door. Zerach got up and opened it and standing in front of him was Demetrius. Demetrius was a demon—a loyal follower of Jaricus, who had also rebelled against Lucifer. Zerach stood in front of him, shock on his face. Demetrius just smiled at him. "Surprised to see me?"

"No, I always knew you would come," said Zerach, balling his fists, preparing himself for attack. "You know, I always thought you were an open-minded person, who did what they wanted. I was wrong; you're still as loyal and foolish as a dog."

"You've got it all wrong, I do what I want and I am loyal only to myself. You, on the other hand, are a boastful fool who is blind by his own arrogance. You're nothing but a pathetic sack of shit whose balls have been dropped off," said Zerach, stepping closer to Demetrius whose eyes were tearing up from anger. "Oh, so you think you can beat me?"

Zerach replied with a smile. "I know I can. In fact, kicking your ass will be child's play."

Demetrius tried to strike Zerach, who blocked his fist. "Is that it? What a fucking joke." Zerach took Demetrius by the hand and flung him out of the window. Demetrius yelled "fuck you" as he fell.

"Alexa, get up. We have to go now." Alexa rose up from the ruckus, not what was going on. "What's happening?"

"No time to explain, just get up and c'mon." Zerach took Alexa by the arm; they ran into an elevator. When the door opened, Zerach was punched in the face and sent flying down the hallway. Demetrius stood in front of Alexa as Zerach laid on the floor, dazed. He came to his senses, then charged Demetrius and crashed through a wall, right in the middle of a couple having sex. Zerach headbutted Demetrius in the face, and then kicked him in the chest. Demetrius fell through another window as he fell. Zerach dove after him. Zerach caught Demetrius in midair with one thrust; Demetrius was slammed to the ground so hard that the concrete was left with his body print. Alexa ran down the stairs, trying to find Zerach. She was frantic, running into people left and right.

Zerach, however, had gained the upper hand on Demetrius, whose body was stunned from being thrown from midair with such tremendous force.

"Tell me why you are so interested in the girl? Huh? What the hell do you want?" said Zerach, his voice rising. "This world is over, the end is already here. Just give it up." Zerach stepped on Demetrius's hand, crushing it. Demetrius yelled in pain, the bone cracked like glass. "You are making a big mistake protecting that girl. She is already dead along with you, angel," said Demetrius, the pain consuming him; the approach of death around the corner. Alexa ran next to Zerach. Demetrius looked over at her and smiled.

"You, girl, are the key to both salvations of good and evil; it all depends if he will get to you," said Demetrius, laughing, while he lay still in the pavement. "Unfortunately for you, salvation will never come your way," replied Zerach, looking down on Demetrius; a crowd gathered around them with eyes as curious as an owl. "Will you ever see salvation?" asked Demetrius in a fit of sarcasm. Zerach knelt down, placed both hands on the face of Demetrius, whose skin began to boil and eyes shatter like glass. Demetrius yelled, his body melting like a Popsicle on a hot day.

Alexa looked on in fear as she could not believe a man had just melted in front of her. "Oh my God! What did you do to him? You just touched him and he—"

Zerach cut her off. "There's no time to explain. We have to go now." He grabbed Alexa by the arm, dragging her to the parking lot. "Please tell me where are we going."

"We're getting away." Zerach hit the gas, speeding out of the parking lot on to the traffic-infested road, making his way like a mouse in a maze. Alexa slouched in her chair, pondering whether or not what she had witnessed was real or just a dream. Zerach sped on to the off ramp, running four cars off the road. Afterward, he parked the car into an abandoned parking lot. Alexa was shaken, torn by these grisly events that have plagued her. Zerach unlocked the car and got out. Alexa got out as well. "Now, do you believe?" asked Zerach putting his hands on her shoulders.

"I'm not sure; I mean what you did to that man."

"He wasn't a man, he was a demon," said Zerach, correcting Alexa.

"Okay, a demon, but still, I've never seen anything like it."

Zerach moved closer toward Alexa and whispered, "Do you still trust me?"

Alexa looked at him with eyes sparkling like water. "Yes, I do." Alexa rested her head against his chest.

Chapter 5

Jaricus was not the only one who had any interest in Alexa. He who was the first angel, Lucifer, also had an interest. Unlike Jaricus, he did not seek her soul for power. Instead, he wanted her dead, for she represented a great threat against his place in hell. In order ensure that Jaricus would not achieve his goal, Lucifer would do anything and everything to prevent it. He would do so without getting his hands dirty. He was walking down the streets of a rundown part of town; the buildings are abandoned and prostitutes were on every corner, as were drug dealers. Down an alley way, Lucifer approached the two doors, and they opened on their own. Two men wearing suits stood by the doors; they each bowed their heads as he was granted entry. The place is packed full of partygoers who are engaging in promiscuous activity, with alcohol, drugs, and sex. They're like damned souls, congregating in a night club. The club was full of lights that changed different colors; the floor was smooth like walking on ice. Lucifer strolled in like he owned the place. One would've thought he did, considering all the people bowed before him. Lucifer was wearing a blue zoot suit with a white tie. The jacket was baby blue and hung down like a trench coat. The bar was filled with people getting drunk and strippers sliding down poles. Lucifer dropped tips on the stage. Two guards stood side by side; Lucifer stared at them with his yellow eyes, and they granted him access inside. Sitting at a desk is a pale man dressed in a red suit. His hair is long and black, resting on his shoulders. His tie looked like a red ribbon around his neck. He has on white pants with brown boots, with a black bet, equipped with a black pistol.

His name is Arius, a drug dealer who sold his soul to Lucifer in exchange for wealth and power. Because of this, he was able to sell as much drugs and make as much money as possible, doing so without ever worrying about being caught. In which he now has the power to buy judges, cops, and politicians. Whenever Lucifer calls upon him for his services, Arius must abridge. Lucifer sat down in a seat. He tapped his finger on the desk to get Arius's attention. "It has been a long time, old friend," said Arius, looking up. "I need you to do something."

"What would you like me to do?" replied Arius.

"I want you to use your connections."

"What for? If I may ask, my lord," said Arius, taking a drink of blood from a wine glass. "There's this girl Alexa; she's caused some trouble for me, and I need you to get rid of her. Right now, she is with a man by the name of Zerachiel," replied Lucifer leaning back in his seat. Arius looked at him, stood up from his seat, and then peered out of a window. "I'll see what I can do; I'll put the word out and have some of my guys do some tracking. I promise I'll make her disappear," replied Arius, turning back at Lucifer.

"Is this Zerachiel her body guard?" asked Arius, sitting down in his seat. "Yeah, and there is someone else who's after her too. He may cause a bit of a problem. So whatever you do, find the girl and kill her fast," said Lucifer, leaning forward in Arius's face.

"Should I be concerned about this other guy?"

"No, don't worry about him, he and I have an old score to settle. Just leave him to me."

"Consider it done. I'll get on it as soon as possible," replied Arius, taking a drink of wine.

"Good, I will keep in touch just in case there is a change of plan," said Lucifer, taking another puff of the cigar. Arius leaned forward and grabbed a cigar from a box that was beside Lucifer. "You seem threatened by this girl?" said Arius in a blunt tone.

"It is not her who is the big problem; she's merely an obstacle. Since I don't take kindly to obstacles, I will simply get rid of her. I know you can make it happen, won't you?" Lucifer got up and walked out. He exited the club, walking off into the night. Meanwhile, Tom was at the precinct, still dealing with the massacre that took place earlier that day. He was examining the names of the victims, wondering why anyone would commit such a horrific crime.

Tom began searching through a high-school yearbook in order to get the names and faces of the victims or possible suspects. He came upon Alexa's photo. Tom immediately called Jason, who was at home spending time with his family.

"Hello."

"Jason, it's me Tom. Come down to the station as soon as you can."

"What's going on?" replied Jason, drenched from swimming with his kids. "I found something you need to see," said Tom, looking at Alexa's picture. "Okay, I'll be there in thirty minutes." Jason hung up the phone, went into his bedroom and got ready, while Tom was still at the precinct running any information in the computer about Alexa.

Jason arrived at the station thirty minutes later. Tom was waiting for him in his office. "This better be good," said Jason, sitting next to Tom. "I found a new lead in the case. I was looking through some photos of the victims at that party. I learned that a girl who attended the party went missing; she was seen fleeing a red corvette with an unknown man." Tom handed the picture to Jason, who analyzed the photo to his astonishment; a witnessed told him her name. "Her name's Alexa."

"How do you know that? You've met her before?"

"No, I spoke to a witness. She said the assailant asked for Alexa who is now missing. I'm assuming the girl in the picture is her," replied Jason, studying the picture closely. "Well, she's apparently been missing for quite some time." Jason looked at Tom, sat back in his seat. "I think this is something we need to look into."

Zerach and Alexa were in the car driving north out of the city limits, trying to get out of the state. Alexa drove comfortably while Zerach rested in the passenger seat, thinking to himself peacefully. "What's it like?" asked Alexa, curious to know more about Zerach.

"What's what like?" Zerach slouched in his seat, turning his eyes on Alexa. "Heaven, what's heaven like?"

"Heaven is peaceful. It's a place of paradise; at least it used to be. Now, it's been divided. Torn by civil war," said Zerach, raising up in his seat.

"Oh, I've always wanted to know what's God like."

Zerach rolled down the window, looking outside as other cars drove next to them. "You're not the only one who's interested in knowing what God is like."

Alexa suddenly hit the brakes as they came across a road block. Police blocked the street, forcing every car to stop and search them for any suspicious activity. Zerach turned the radio on. "Breaking news, the manhunt is on for a mysterious couple suspected of being involved of the massacre that took place at a party just yesterday."

"Oh shit. What do we do?" asked Alexa frantically. "We stay cool. Just drive through and be calm. I promise we'll be okay," replied Zerach. They eased their way up to the stop as a police officer approached the driver side. "License and registration."

"Is there a problem, Officer?" asked Zerach.

"Just doing a routine check."

"Okay. Is everything okay, Officer?" Zerach repeated himself, only this time, the officer was in a trance; his eyes are dilated, his entire body stiff. "Like I said before, there is no problem, sorry to trouble you. You're free to pass through. Here's your license and registration," said the officer. "Thank you very much." Zerach said, smiling at Alexa. They drove through road block without any obstructions.

"What did you do to him?"

"I guess he realized there wasn't a problem. Wait, pull over!" Alexa pulled the car over on the side of the road. "Keep the gas running."

"What's wrong?" Zerach turned to her. "Alexa, stay in the car." He could sense something nearby; it wasn't Jaricus. In fact, it was something more powerful. Zerach could feel the demonic energy coming closer, closing in on his mind and body. The object came crashing down like a wave of water rampaging through a forest. It could be only one thing—Lucifer. Only a demon such as he can possess an energy so high the clouds roar and a power so vast the earth shakes. In cloud of white smoke, the devil himself appeared in front of Zerach. "Hello, little brother. Excited to see me?" Zerach took a step back, having no clue to why Lucifer was here. "What brings you here?" asked Zerach, feeling nervous, knowing he might not be a match for Lucifer. "I have a little problem, and I have to stop it before it becomes a big problem. As they say, if you want something done, then you have to do it yourself. That brings me to her," said Lucifer, pointing at Alexa.

"The girl has nothing to do with you."

"As a matter of fact, she does have every bit to do with me because she is the key to making an enemy of mine a god. Something I cannot allow."

"Jaricus is the one you're after?"

"Precisely," replied Lucifer, folding his arms.

"Then why not kill him, let the girl live."

"I suppose I could, but I prefer to play it safe." Zerach lunged at Lucifer, who in turn struck him down with a force of invisible energy.

"Run!" Zerach yelled at Alexa as Lucifer lifted him off the ground, throwing him into a tree. Alexa got out of the car, running to Zerach's aid when Lucifer grabbed her by the hair. He held her up one hand and a knife in the other. Zerach rushed to him, kicking Lucifer in the back of the head. "You okay?" said Zerach, holding Alexa. Before she had a chance to respond, Zerach was lit with rays of demonic energy and nearly crushed by the force of impact. He opened his arms using his power to suck the energy within him and then fired it back at Lucifer.

The devil hit the floor, the ground cracking as he hit. "Nice move, I didn't see that coming," said Lucifer, rising up to challenge Zerach again. "You know you're no match for me."

"Don't forget I've beaten you before," replied Zerach, wielding two swords in his hands.

"Yeah, that was only one time and you got lucky. Now it's time to die." Lucifer rushed Zerach with tremendous speed, as Zerach didn't have a chance to get a swing of his swords. Whisked into the sky and back down to the pavement, Zerach got back up. He and Lucifer took to the skies. In one leap, they fought in midair, Zerach lashing out with his swords and Lucifer dodging every attack. Zerach clamped the two blades together as they formed one sword. Lucifer attempted to block the attack but was struck through the stomach. Both of them came back down, landing on their feet. Zerach's sword covered in Lucifer's blood, the mighty demon held his hand over his abdomen. "Lucky strike, now it's time to get down." Lucifer pulled fire from his hands as if it came from the depths of hell itself. Zerach prepared himself for the oncoming attack. He crossed his sword in front of him to create a shield. Lucifer launched the flames at Zerach, who is consumed by them. "Zerach!" yelled Alexa, getting out of the car. She was scared Zerach may be dead. Zerach burst through the flames with all his might, his sword in hand, wielding it like a rope over his head.

With one slash, the blade ejected a piece of energy resembling a boomerang at Lucifer. The ring of energy was a blade, cutting off Lucifer's arm; and then Zerach threw another, cutting off Lucifer's second arm. "Is that it? That's all you possess?" Lucifer smiled as two new arms grew back. "I possess enough to kill you!" exclaimed Zerach, leaping into the air, diving down toward the devil and his heart, with the sword over his head ready to cut off some meat. Lucifer tried to freeze him, but Zerach dodged the attack, coming down faster and harder with the sword. Lucifer jumped out of the way when Zerach crashed down on the pavement. The sound from the impact was so staggering that the ground shook. Lucifer smiled with arrogance. He leaned back, folded his arms and said, "Now that was fun. But today is the wrong day to kill you. I prefer to have a worthy audience. Good day, Zerach." Lucifer turned into dust and blew away with the wind. Zerach put his swords away, knowing exactly why Lucifer fled.

"Are you okay?" asked Alexa, worried with sweat.

"I'm fine. We need to go now." They got back into the car, driving off into the distance.

Meanwhile, Tom and Jason were at the precinct, speaking to homicide detectives in regards to the massacre. The room had a round table where the detectives sat. The walls were white, freshly painted, and a large white board bolted on a wall in the front of the room. Tom sat down with a clipboard, along with the other detectives, while Jason presented the case. "Now, you all know about a few days ago there was a massacre that took place. There were a dozen victims. We have the bodies and DNA samples. What we don't have are suspects." Jason posted a picture of Alexa on the board. "Her name is Alexa. She went missing the night of the murders. She was last seen at a gas station with this man; he is unknown, but we believe they had something to do with the murders that took place. We are going to have to work fast to bring these two in for questioning." Jason left the pictures up on the board and headed into the next room for coffee. Tom walked in behind him, holding some papers. "So when do we start? Because I'm ready to catch the son of a bitch."

Jason took a sip of his coffee; he sat it down and said, "Whoa there, this case needs to be handled with a little ease, okay? Especially with your reputation as a hot head."

"C'mon, I'm a good cop. I'm Calm." Jason looked at Tom with a look of gasp. "Tom, you put two priests in custody for baptizing any eight-year-old boy."

"So what? They baptizing some kids doesn't mean they weren't going to molest them," Jason snarled and kept sipping his coffee. Tom sat on the counter, opening a bottle of water.

"So where do we begin?" asked Tom in a cocky tone of voice.

"Well, we start by asking some questions, and if anything pops up, we'll be on it."

On the other side of town, Jaricus was soaring the skies in the form of a crow, scanning the city with a bird's eye view, smelling the air for a teenage girl who is his salvation for tremendous power. Black wings stretched out as the wind carried him through the clouds. A bright light caught the demon's eye. Jaricus dove down, his eyes fixed like radar and the clouds bursting apart; lightning radiating the sky. Jaricus landed on a roof of a church. He came back into his original form, standing tall, listening to the chorus as they sang to their god, praising him till their breaths broke. Jaricus was disgusted by the worship; he felt sickened to his stomach, his teeth grinded together. "Listen to them! It's despicable." Jaricus punched through the roof, causing it to melt. A fire irrupted, and the roof was a blaze. Beneath him, Jaricus could hear the people as they screamed. Their screams were music to his ears with a foul smile. "Burn." The church burned until it was reduced to ashes. All that was left were the charred remains of the people attending the church service. Jaricus floated to the ground, his coat blowing in the wind, his eyes red as cherries. His long hair blew with the breeze. The flames burned behind him, and it seemed Jaricus had risen from hell, and hell followed him. Jaricus stood calm, collected, while gazing at the street. The cops were on the scene, as well as the fire department and paramedics. A police officer got out of his car; he said, "Put your hands on your head. And move slowly forward." A SWAT team pulled up, surrounding the perimeter alongside the other officers. Jaricus stood motionless, his black hair resting on his shoulders. "I will not ask you again, put your hands on your head or we will fire!"

Jaricus did not budge, standing still as a rock. The cops fired their weapons. Jaricus was hit by the bullets, his flesh pierced by the thousands of hot lead. His body fell to the ground like a statue falling to pieces. "Hold your fire." The cops stopped shooting. They think it is done, but what they don't know is Jaricus is far from dead. Jaricus rises from the ground, healing himself involuntarily right back to his full state.

"That was good. Now it's my turn." Jaricus raised hit coat wide open; they looked like wings and shrouded the scene. Hundreds of demonic ravens flew from Jaricus's coat, appearing from his flesh, flying straight toward the officers. "WHAT THE FUCK!" the cops yelled, running as they fired their weapons, which had no effect. The ravens sneered, tore chunks of flesh off the officers bones. The ravens shrieked loud enough, the windows on the cars broke. The ravens were like piranhas ripping their prey to shreds in seconds, leaving nothing but bones. The fire behind him grew until it surrounded him. Jaricus began to walk on the air, the tortured souls around him; his grin and eyes shined in the night. A giant shroud of souls attached to his back like a cape blew behind him. People tried to run, but there is no escape. Jaricus's serpents of hell were unleashed, devouring every mortal. Jaricus looked to the skies.

"Who's the god now?" He laughed the most sinister laugh ever heard by human ears. There seemed to be no end to his terror; only one question remained—can anything stop him?

Chapter 6

Zerach and Alexa were still on the run. Their car was running low on gas, plus it had been damaged from their previous encounter with Demetrius.

"We need to find a new car." Zerach pulled over. Alexa was a sleep, awakened by what Zerach said.

"What?"

"I said we need a new car. This one's done." Zerach pulled the car over on a curb. He and Alexa got out of the car when it started raining. "Great. Now, what are we going to do?" said Alexa, frustrated.

"We walk," replied Zerach, putting his coat around Alexa.

"Walk? Great, just when my luck couldn't get any worse. Where are we going, by the way?"

"We are going someplace safe; a place where they can't get to you. It's a place no demon can cross," said Zerach, putting his arm around Alexa.

"Tell me, why are you protecting me?"

"I chose to protect you."

"What?" replied Alexa, curious as to why Zerach would make such a decision.

"I chose to protect you because I wanted to. I felt it was my duty to do so." Zerach ran his fingers through Alexa's hair as she placed her hand on his cheek. Zerach turned away shyly, uncomfortable with the thought of having feelings for Alexa. "What are you afraid of?" asked Alexa, putting her hands on his shoulders, trying to comfort him. "We need to get out of here," Zerach said, grabbing Alexa's hands. A guy on a chopper drove past them and pulled into a parking lot. Zerach smiled and said, "I just found us a ride." Alexa looked at the guy on the motorcycle; Zerach approached him with ease. The man on the bike was a member of the Hell's Angels. He had the vest with the patch and a beard like Santa Clause. "Sorry to trouble you, but I was wondering if I could have your bike?" The guy looked at Zerach and said, "Is that a fucking joke?"

"No, it's not." Zerach focused his thoughts on to the biker's mind. The biker began to sweat and fall into a zombie state. "Now, get off the bike and give me the key."

The biker responded in a dry tone, "Here is my key . . . and I will walk away." The biker gave up the key then started walking away when Zerach suddenly forgot something. "Aren't you forgetting something?" The biker came back, took off his helmet and gave it to Zerach. "Now, go and keep walking until you can walk no more." With that being said, the biker, still under Zerach's control, turned around and walked until he could no longer be seen.

"What did you do to him?" asked Alexa.

"I just told him to give me his bike, so he did."

"Right," replied Alexa, putting on the helmet, sitting behind Zerach. "Hold on tight, it may get a little rough." Zerach hit the gas speeding off into the street, Alexa holding on for dear life.

"Where are we going?"

"Somewhere safe. I have an old friend waiting for us." Alexa held on tight, her arms wrapped around Zerach's waste, her hair blowing in the wind. Alexa was at peace; she could feel Zerach's warmth and knew that as long as she had him, everything will be fine.

Meanwhile, Tom and Jason arrived on the scene where Jaricus left behind a path of monstrous destruction, one that no one can comprehend. They got out of the car with shock and horror on their faces, in disbelief on what lay before them. The streets were littered with toppled cars and trucks, the buildings were so damaged they looked like ruins. A crater a mile deep rested in the middle of the ground, and the bodies of officers and civilians lay on the ground. The bodies were cold and still like rock, their mouths gaping open. Their eyes were gone, their sockets were completely empty. Jaricus had devoured their souls.

"My god," whispered Jason, shocked by what was in front of him. He walked on the side where soulless corpses lay, burning cars toppled and crushed all around him. "What happened?" Jason asked an officer who was one of the first to arrive. "They got a call about a bombing, and the suspect stood about fifty feet away on that post. I don't know how to say this, but he used some sort of supernatural magic or something."

"What do you mean?" asked Jason, confused.

"I mean, he summoned some sort of demon shit I don't know!" said the cop, his voice cracking with fear.

"All right, relax. Why don't you go ahead and get checked out by the paramedics, okay?"

"Jason, come here quick!" yelled Tom, who was standing in the middle of the street.

"What is it?"

"Check this. You recognize something?" Tom said, pointing to the ground. "Recognize what?" asked Jason. Tom pointed down at the ground, and to his amazement, the symbol they found at the massacre was imbedded into the ground a mile wide. "What the hell? That's the same cross we found at the last crime scene," said Jason in disbelief. "I know this sounds crazy, but who did all of this is the same guy or people responsible for the massacre," said Tom with excitement on his face. "Shit! Well, for now, get everything cleaned up, collect as much evidence as you can find, and talk to witnesses." Jason walked back to the car; Tom followed him and got on the driver's side. "Jason, what do you think? Satanic cult? Terrorists?"

"I don't know, kiddo. Whatever it is, it's still out there and we need to find it or them." Suddenly, a tall building about two hundred yards away from them exploded. "Holy shit!" Yelled Tom. "Back up quick!" exclaimed Jason. The building was engulfed in flames, dupery and chunks of concrete fell from the sky like rain, crushing everything in its path. The fire looked like clouds, merging as one giant inferno. People still trapped inside, were falling like leaves from a tall tree. "What the fuck is going on?" exclaimed Tom, going in reverse, swerving around, trying to outrun the dupery as it crashed like thunder after them.

"Get on the curve!" said Jason, looking behind him, wondering if the world was coming to an end. Tom sped on the curve, while sirens behind them thundered down the street toward the blaze of fire. The building was nothing but ash and ruin, as Jason caught a glimpse of Jaricus standing within the inferno.

"Who the hell is that?" Jason said to himself. Jaricus stood staring right back at Jason, with eyes as if fixed on him as a lion fixes on its prey. Jaricus turned and disappeared without a trace. "I think we're definitely dealing with some terrorist," said Tom, stopping the car, getting out to catch his breath. "I saw someone. He was standing in the fire," said Jason, stunned by what he witnessed. "Sir, who'd you see?"

"It was a man. I saw him, then he was gone."

"Who?"

"Shit, I don't know. But all I know is he looked right at me. He saw me."

Zerach and Alexa were on the road until Zerach pulled over to a sudden stop. "What's wrong?" asked Alexa, seeing the wide-eyed look on Zerach. "I just heard the voices of thousands scream as if they were right next to me." Alexa got off the bike, checking if Zerach was okay. "What do you mean voices?"

"It's Jaricus; he killed all those people for no reason at all. We have to keep moving. I have to get you to where the others are and face him alone."

"Why do you have to face him alone?" asked Alexa. "Because I can't fight him with you in the way. I'll worry about you too much. Get on." Zerach hit the gas, and they were off to where Zerach's allies awaited him in a large secure fortress. Zerach was able to sense Jaricus's energy, and he knew that if he could feel Jaricus's energy, then Jaricus could feel his as well. They rode off into the sunset, trying to buy time, for time was something they were running out of. By now, Jaricus is searching far and wide feeding off the energy he sensed was so familiar. He knew that if he found Zerach, he will find Alexa, for he was more anxious than usual. Now Jaricus was more powerful than ever before, thanks to the new souls he drained during his tirade. He now displayed even more confidence in defeating Zerach and, above all, winning Alexa's soul.

Jaricus couldn't help but laugh at the thought, for he knew in his heart that once Alexa was his, there will be no stopping him. His goal of becoming a god may come true. He was flying, his wings outstretched. Lightning followed him as he soared above the ground. Jaricus could taste the energy he felt from Zerach, and now he was getting closer. Zerach was feeling Jaricus's presence deepen and coming faster. Jaricus could smell Alexa; her sent is getting stronger and stronger, giving him even more drive. Zerach was doing a hundred on a sixty-five-mile-per-hour road; Alexa hung to him for dear life. Jaricus approached closer, he could see them; he was gaining even faster. Zerach hit the gas harder; Jaricus could hear the engine. His excitement grew like a child awaiting a birthday gift. Jaricus could see them; he swooped down like a hawk chasing a mouse.

Zerach hit the break, catching Alexa as she nearly fell off the bike. Jaricus stood in front of them like a deer caught in the headlights.

"Hello, Zerach. Did you miss me? 'Cause I sure missed you and that pretty little lady behind you."

"Alexa, get off," Zerach told Alexa, who was shaking from fear.

"What about you, what are you going to do?"

"Don't worry about me. Just get off the bike and find cover. It'll be over soon, trust me."

"Oh, it will be over soon because you'll be the one screaming in intense agony from pain upon which you have never felt in your life," Jaricus said, cracking his knuckles; Zerach pulled daggers from his sleeves. Jaricus retracted his wings into him, then he wielded two pistols and pulled the triggers. Zerach threw the daggers; the bullets and knives collided. Zerach was struck by the bullets and was thrown to the ground. The knives pierced Jaricus's chest and stomach; he too hit the ground. They lay there motionless for a few minutes until they got back up fully rejuvenated. Jaricus pulled the knives out of his chest, dropping them to the ground and then stepping on them. Zerach pushed the bullets out of his flesh by simply flexing his muscles; his body then healed itself in seconds. Jaricus had his pistols in his hands, flipping them like the cowboys did in the western movies.

"Since when were you a fucking cowboy?" said Zerach, adjusting himself. "Since today. I'm going to kill you." Jaricus ran toward Zerach, this time, wielding a sword, which pulled his sword as well. Charging each other like speed trains, they collided; spurs of angelic and demonic energy swept the landscape. Alexa duct behind a tree stump surrounded by tall green grass. The energy was like a gust of wind comprised of intense heat. Chunks of grass and boulders blew out of the ground, the road cracked. Jaricus threw Zerach in the air, then leaped after him. Zerach tried to regain control. Jaricus had his sword in hand, the blade aimed at his chest. It merged into Zerach, who tried desperately to ignore the pain. "Do you like that?" said Jaricus, piercing Zerach's chest inches from his heart. "Time to die!" Jaricus used his blade to fling Zerach to the ground, and the impact was so great it left a body print of Zerach on the road. Zerach stumbled to his feet, Jaricus free fell toward Zerach. His sword aimed right at him. Jaricus came down and right before the blade hit its target. Zerach dodged the attack using a new and difficult move. He used an out-of-body technique where can use his spirit as way to be in two places at once.

"Is that it? That's all you've got? Because if it is, I'm very disappointed," said Zerach, his wounds already heeled. "Zerach, that was just an appetizer, allow me to show you the main course." Jaricus prepared for another attack, taking the offensive, he dove after Zerach. He flipped over Jaricus, dodging the attack. As Jaricus turned around, Zerach took his hands and shot Jaricus with a beam of hot energy into his face.

Jaricus flew back, skidding across the pavement. Zerach threw another ball of energy, another then another, until Jaricus was completely surrounded in a huge cluster. An explosion occurred, and once the smoke cleared, Jaricus could not be seen anywhere. Zerach looked around trying to sense where Jaricus was, but nothing. Alexa was still knelt behind the stump which was covered by tall grass. "Alexa! Are you okay?"

"Yeah, I'm fine," replied Alexa, standing up not knowing that Jaricus was behind her. "Alexa, run!" shouted Zerach, but it was too late. Alexa screamed as Jaricus snatched her by the hair, putting his sword to her throat. "Got ya! Well, that was easy. Whoa! Calm down, no need to be feisty. Now, what a pickle we got ourselves here. Zerach, what will you do now?" Zerach stood still, restless, knowing if he made any advancement toward

Alexa, Jaricus would kill her. "Jaricus, you're making a huge mistake. You're better off letting her go."

"You know I don't want to; instead, I'm going to make proper use of her and do what I came here to do. I know that you'll pursue me if I take off. You kill me, she dies with me." Zerach took a small step forward; Jaricus tightened his grip on Alexa.

Zerach pulled a dagger from his sleeve. He turned around then faced Jaricus again, and he threw the dagger as quick as he could. Jaricus was caught by surprise and was struck in the forehead. He hit the floor, and Alexa ran into Zerach's arms. "Are you okay?"

"I'm fine"

"Let's go; we have to move fast." Zerach and Alexa got on the motorcycle and sped off as fast as they could. Jaricus stood up and pulled the burning dagger out of his head; the pain was exuviating because the blade was dipped in holy water. "Bastard." Jaricus was back on his feet and needed some transportation. To his luck, a big rig was driving up. Jaricus smirked. He stood in front of the truck as it came to a sudden halt. Jaricus leaped on to the hood of the car; the guy driving the truck freaked out and ran. Jaricus got in and hit the gas, following Zerach's trail. He hit the gas; the big rig began picking up momentum. Zerach and Alexa are gunning it to their destination. Looking in the side mirror, Zerach could see Jaricus coming closer. "Alexa, I'm going to need to get off the bike." Zerach made a quick stop on the side of the road. "Zerach, what are you going to do?"

"You'll see."

"Just don't get hurt," replied Alexa standing to the side. Zerach turned the bike headed for a collision course with Jaricus. "You play a game of chicken with me, boy! Hah!" yelled Jaricus, pressing down on the pedal even harder. Jaricus and Zerach were both headed for each other with no intention of moving out of the way. Zerach had his weapon drawn, the blade scraping against the cement, cutting through it like butter. Jaricus was determined to crush Zerach to pieces. They got closer and closer. Jaricus aimed the truck like a guided missile; Zerach maneuvered around the truck, cutting the side of it with his blade, causing the truck to tip over. Zerach slid his motorcycle under the truck, crashing on the side of the road into a tree. Jaricus, still trapped in, punched through the door; but as soon as he did, the truck blew up. His body, engulfed in flames, flew into the clouds. Alexa covered her head from the flames and Dupree. The truck burned as it was covered in an inferno, the smoke blocking out the sun, creating a sky of grey treachery. Zerach lay on the ground motionless, face down on the ground, his swords by his side. Alexa got up. She walked through the thick smoke, covering her nose and mouth with her coat. She ran to Zerach's side, seeing him lying down on the ground. "Zerach!" Alexa crouched down, putting her hands on his back, nudging him. "Zerach, please get up, please!" Alexa was frantic; she turned him over, putting his head in her lap. "Zerach, wake up!" said Alexa panicking, hoping for some sign Zerach is alive. "Zerach, I know you can hear. Just please get up!"

Zerach got up, dazed, holding his head. Zerach shook off the pain and got up. "I'm fine. Jaricus isn't dead." He rose up, looking at the flames. "We need to get out of here now."

"Jaricus went up in flames. I doubt he'll be coming back anytime soon," replied Alexa, dusting Zerach off, making sure he was okay. "I know it will only slow him down. Shit! We need some wheels," said Zerach. He and Alexa were walking off until sirens could be heard. Just out in the horizon were flashing lights, an ambulance and police cars coming their way. "Dammit! What do we do now?" asked Alexa, turning to Zerach, not sure what to do. "We'll let them take us. I'll think of something later." The cops and ambulance surrounded them. "Put your hands on your heads!"

"Put your hands where I can see them!" Zerach looked at Alexa with a smile. "It's going to be fine, trust me."

"Okay, whatever you say." Alexa was approached by a cop. She was handcuffed and taken to a car. She had been placed in the back seat and was scared because she had never been in a situation like this before. Zerach was also handcuffed. He kept his cool, allowing the police to do their job. They padded him down, retrieving all his weapons; they were shocked by the discovery. A fire truck pulled up; the firefighters got out, pulled out the hose and hooked them up to the truck. The firefighters sprayed down the big rig, putting out the flames. Zerach and Alexa were driven to a hospital to treat any wounds; the funny thing was, they had no wounds. The drive to the nearest hospital was a little ways away, so Alexa decided to take the time to think about all that has happened to her thus far. All the events that have taken place can never make any sense to Alexa. She sat back, sighed, and worried not for herself but for Zerach. Zerach was her one and only reason to exist; without him there is no her. The ride in the back of the cop car was nerve-racking; the seats were uncomfortable and Alexa kept fidgeting. She kept looking behind her, trying to see Zerach.

Zerach, on the other hand, kept his mind off the drive. His focus was on Alexa, preparing himself for Jaricus's next move which may happen at any time. About an hour had gone by and they finally arrived at a police station. An officer was talking through a radio. The officer said, "We have them. Yes, they're in custody, both of them." At that moment, Tom and Jason were in their car when they received the news. "Okay, roger that. Holy shit! They got 'em. I just spoke to the captain at the next county; they said they have the man and the girl," said Tom, nearly jumping out of his seat. Jason looked at him with some relief. "Where are they located?"

"North right over that hill." Tom pointed straight ahead. "I can't believe it. Finally, we can put all this mess behind us," said Tom, excited over the moment. "Don't get your hopes up; we still need to ask some questions," Jason butted in, ruining Tom's celebration. "C'mon, you know these two did it. Besides it's only common sense."

"Well, look at you, hotshot! We've haven't even met them and already you think you have this case solved," said Jason, laughing at Tom who was now taking the situation seriously. They pulled into the parking lot, got out, and into character. Jason led the way, with Tom not too far behind him. They entered the department building. Jason and Tom were both greeted by an attractive secretary whom Tom had an eye for. "Hello, the captain has been expecting you."

"Thank you. Can you tell us where his office is located?" asked Tom in a flirtatious whisper. "It's just down the hall," replied the secretary, smiling. Tom and Jason head north of where the secretary's desk was into the captain's office. "Come on in," said the captain.

"Hi, we're—"

"I know who you are. You're here for the man and young woman." Jason stepped forward. "Yes, we are. We would like to ask them some questions."

"Okay, no problem. Name's James. Right this way." The captain was a chunky man, tall, with a bald head and large, protruding stomach. He had on a pair of glasses that were silver. His name was James; Capt. James is what people called him.

"My men got a call about an explosion and who'd of thought we'd run into these two," James said, chuckling.

"Thanks for your help, Captain. Now all we need to do is get some answers," said Jason. Tom butted in, "Let's do this. I'm ready to nail these crackpots. I'll get the guy."

"All right, fine. James, thanks for everything."

"My pleasure. I'll just be on the other side of the interrogation room." Zerach sat calmly still; he could hear and see the men talking through the walls. He could also hear Alexa's heart beating in the next room, sensing she's nervous. Alexa sat in her seat, taking a sip of water out of a cup. She was scared, not knowing if she would spend the rest of her life behind bars. The door swung open; in came Jason with a pen and notepad. He was cool and collected; Alexa could tell he's done this before.

"Hi, how are you?" asked Jason, sitting across from Alexa. Alexa didn't respond; she sat there speechless. "My name is Jason. I work for the LAPD. I just want to ask you a few questions." Alexa nodded her head.

"Good. For starters, would you like anything to drink? Water, soda, a cup of coffee?" Alexa shook her head. "I'm sure you heard about the murders that took place a few days ago at a party? It was in all the major news outlets."

"Yeah, I heard of it," Alexa replied nervously. Jason sat back and took out a cigar. "You mind if I smoke?"

"No, it's fine with me."

"Okay. Well, the reason why I asked you about the murders is because I was told you were there when it all happened. Is this true?" Alexa was going to answer, but she began to quiver and stutter. "It's fine, just want to know the truth," said Jason, calm and cool. Alexa kept stuttering, not knowing what to say. Finally, she let it all out. "There was this guy, he was trying to kill me."

"What's this guy's name?"

"He said his name was Jaricus. He killed my best friend Jennifer." Alexa folded her arms, slouched in her seat.

"Tell me about the man you've been traveling with; did he kidnap you?"

"Zerach didn't kidnap me; he saved me."

Jason looked up. "His name is Zerach? What did you know about him prior to him saving you?"

"I didn't know him, I had no idea who he was," said Alexa, looking around nervously. "So why would you go with him and not call the police if you had no clue or knew nothing about him?" Jason asked condescendingly.

"What was I supposed do? I—" "Well, call the police. Instead you decided to run off with a complete stranger."

"No, he saved my life."

"Didn't anything click in your head that he may not be trustworthy? I mean, you didn't know who he was until that night."

"You have to know something; this guy Jaricus, he's trying to kill me. Zerach and I have been trying to get away from him." Jason leaned back. "And why does he want to kill you?"

"If I told you, you'd think I was crazy," said Alexa, slouching further in her seat.

"Go ahead, tell me."

Alexa took a deep breath. "It's complicated."

"Why is it complicated?"

"It just is! Okay?" snapped Alexa.

"All right, calm down. I was just asking a simple question, that's all." There was a knock at the door. Tom comes in enthusiastic, more than usual.

"Hey, the other suspect is in the other room; the guy looks like a real nut case." Jason turned to him. "Let me guess, you want to interrogate him yourself."

"You read my mind." Tom and Jason walked out of the room where Alexa was and into the room where Zerach was sitting quietly. "Sir, I'm telling you, this guy did it, and she's protecting him."

"Don't go on making assumptions; we don't have any concrete evidence to get them in front of a jury."

"I know that, sir, but I got a good feeling that we got the person responsible."

"All right, all right, you can do it. But try not to do anything reckless, okay?" said Jason, putting his finger in Tom's face.

"Thank you, sir." Tom walked into the interrogation room where Zerach sat relaxed and quite comfortable in a seat. Tom sat across from him in character, ready to interrogate. "Hi, my name is Tom—"

"Tom, I know who you are," said Zerach, leaning back in his chair. Tom was overcome with surprise.

"What did you say?"

"I said I know who you are, Tom."

Tom rolled up his sleeves, determined to get any answers he could get out of Zerach. "You listen to me; tell me anything you know about the massacre."

"What massacre?"

"You know which one I'm talking about."

"Actually, I'm not quite sure if I do," Zerach said, playing stupid. "Don't bullshit me! The fucking massacre that took place three days ago!" Zerach leaned forward. "Oh that massacre. Now I remember."

"Yeah, what do you know about it?"

"All I know is there's not much time." Zerach stood up, pushed the chair back into the table, and clenched his fists.

"What the hell are you doing? Sit down!"

"He's here," said Zerach in a low voice.

"Who's here? Was there anyone else involved?"

"Get down!" The walls exploded, flames engulfed the entire building, and Zerach could see a figure flying toward him. It was Jaricus. He tackled Zerach, smashing through a wall, then another and another. They were both fighting in midair, free falling hundreds of feet high above the ground. Jaricus punched Zerach in the face continuously.

"It's over!" yelled Jaricus. Zerach grabbed his hand, kneed him in the balls, and headbutted him. "It's over for you!" yelled Zerach, kicking Jaricus into another building. Jaricus crashed through the building like a plane. Zerach landed on a window; he kicked it in and then dropped and kicked Jaricus into a bathroom. "Jaricus, I've had enough! You'll never get her." Jaricus stood up, staring Zerach in the eyes.

"You're wrong. After I kill you, I'm going to paint her face with your blood!" Jaricus kicked Zerach through another wall. Onlookers stood in the building, watching in astonishment at what they were witnessing. Jaricus pulled a whip from his coat that had spikes serving around it. He slashed the whip at Zerach, who dodged the lash. Instead, Jaricus had lashed a man in half. The people still in the building ran for their lives. Jaricus whipped the whip back again and again. Zerach moved out of the way just in time.

"C'mon, angel, I know this isn't your best." Jaricus slashed the whip again; Zerach caught it in his hands. They both pulled on the whip. Zerach's hands were bleeding, but he ignored the pain and focused his energy on Jaricus. Jaricus pulled the whip, cutting Zerach's hands then wrapping it around his neck. Jaricus twirled him around like a rag doll then darted out of the window, running down the side of the building, dragging Zerach behind him. Jaricus flung the whip, and Zerach went flying down the building like a skydiver.

Alexa, who was back at the interrogation room, stood up and looked at both Tom and Jason. "I told you it was complicated."

Jaricus dove after Zerach, slashing the whip at him again. Zerach caught it, tugged on it in midair, and launched himself back up, landing a fist into

Jaricus's face. Jaricus grabbed Zerach by the leg and threw him up the towering building. Jaricus leaped after him, this time drawing his sword. Zerach regained himself and then planted his feet onto the cemented wall of the building, drawing his swords as well. They clashed, wielding their swords like ninjas. Zerach wailed away at Jaricus, who intern blocked every attack. Jaricus managed to knock one sword out Zerach's hands; it fell until it was stuck into the side of the building. Jaricus stabbed Zerach in the chest. "Time to die!" said Jaricus, flinging Zerach in the air and then slashing him with his blade. Zerach fell from the sky, plummeting down to the ground. As Zerach fell, he tried to regain consciousness; his heart began to pound faster, his eyes opened wide with silver. With one of his swords still in his hand, he stuck in the building's cement. He stood on the blade like a soldier. Zerach raised his hand and the other sword came to him like a magnet. Zerach leaped down, put the swords together, forming one weapon. Jaricus looked upon him with confusion. Zerach's wings came from under his skin; they were stretched to their fullest.

Alexa was running down a hallway, Tom and Jason behind her. They could see Zerach and Jaricus fighting on a building. The building they were in had a gaping hole the size of a freeway tunnel. "C'mon, call for back up," said Jason.

"What about the girl?"

"Take her with us." Alexa was yanked by Tom and was forced to go with them. "I'm not leaving without Zerach!" Tom looked at her. "You don't have a choice, now c'mon!" Alexa went with Tom and Jason down the stairs to the parking lot, which was the only part not harmed.

Zerach and Jaricus continued their battle. Zerach flew toward Jaricus like a bat out of hell, clipping Jaricus with his wing; Jaricus was knocked off the building and slid down as if on a slide. Zerach gained air and then swooped down after him with a vengeance. Zerach stabbed the blade into Jaricus's chest. Zerach lifted him up in the air. Jaricus's blood ran down the blade. "Your days have ended," said Zerach. Jaricus stared at him, with blood running down his nose; in a choking tone he said, "Zerach, you're nothing but a puppet. A mere plaything to serve your master." Jaricus chuckled. Zerach, enveloped with anger, flung Jaricus to the sky. Zerach flew after him. Jaricus regained his strength, looked down and saw Zerach with his sword in hand, ready to make the final blow. Jaricus delivered a clever move—he teleported, disappearing before Zerach's eyes.

Zerach stopped in midair, his wings still open, searching for Jaricus, anticipating his next move. "What's the matter? Can't see me?" Jaricus's voice came from nowhere. Zerach swung his sword, he hit nothing but air. Jaricus struck Zerach like a bolt of lightning thrown by Zeus. Jaricus struck Zerach again. This time, he was falling from the sky, headed toward the ground below. Jaricus nosedived after him, colliding with him. "You see that, Zerach? That is your demise!" They both hit the ground, hitting the busy street. Cars and pedestrians were blown off the road. Debris filled the air, cars were toppled, people lay dead or wounded. Screams of people and car alarms was all that could be heard. Jaricus arose, feeling victorious. Zerach lay in the cratered ground, dazed, unsure where he was. Zerach retracted his wings into his back, stumbling to his feet. Jaricus charged him, swinging his sword at Zerach's head. He missed. Zerach went for Jaricus's legs, but Jaricus jumped into the air. Zerach followed, determined to finish the fight.

They locked blades; Jaricus put his hand in front of Zerach's face, blasted him with a hand of fire. Zerach fell back, falling fast to the ground. He landed on his feet, causing the ground to tear. Jaricus jumped up, his blade aimed for Zerach's heart, he came down like a falcon. The wind whistled as he broke through the sky's barrier, closer he came. Jaricus could hear Zerach's heart pumping. Jaricus was just inches away; Zerach timed the moment when it was right. He pulled his sword. Jaricus landed, only being blocked, foiling his attempt. Zerach pushed upward and then kicked Jaricus in the stomach. Jaricus swung his sword, locking with Zerach's again.

"You're not as weak as the other angels, but you're still not strong enough to kill me," said Jaricus.

"I have enough power to kill you!" They broke free, both of them clashing their swords like savage beasts. Alexa was in the back seat of a cop car Tom was driving, with Jason in the passenger seat. Cop cars behind them, they were driving through traffic, sirens ringing out. People darting out of the way, some were watching the epic fight between Zerach and

Jaricus. "Watch it!" yelled Jason. "All units, stay close. Keep an eye on the suspects. Whatever you do, apprehend them at all costs!"

"Hold on." Tom hit the gas, and the car jumped into high gear. Jaricus noticed the car coming toward him and Zerach. "What's this?" then took off toward the car.

"Watch him," said Jason, bracing himself. "I got you, you son of a—" Jaricus leaped over the car. Jaricus opened his hand, shooting out flames of hell, blowing up the cop cars that had been following Tom, Jason, and Alexa.

"Jesus!" yelled Tom, skidding down the street. People ran in all directions, as the flames upon which Jaricus created had taken hold on downtown Los Angeles. Cars and small shops were in flames. "Well, it looks like I got a little carried away," said Jaricus, smirking at Zerach. "You are a bastard."

"Why, thank you; I take pleasure in playing that role."

Zerach attacked Jaricus, slashing his sword more ferociously than before. Jaricus jumped into the air, Zerach was in pursuit, barely missing Jaricus's head. Zerach and Jaricus landed on the roof of a burning building. Suddenly, the sky turned grey, lightning pierced the air, and rain fell from above. The water and fire looked like a spectacle; it was as if heaven and hell were merging on earth, seeming as though the world had catapulted itself in this disarray not being able to free itself from man, trying to find its identity. "This rain is perfect for your demise, Jaricus," said Zerach, water running down his face. "There is no end for me; only conquest is my fate. Now die!" Jaricus swung his sword. Zerach jumped in the air, coming down. Jaricus moved out of the way; Zerach's blade went through the roof. Jaricus rushed to Zerach and kicked the sword out of his hands. Zerach, now unarmed, was face to face with a demon and its sword from hell.

Jaricus laughed. "What's the matter, fire of God?" Jaricus raised his blade up high, coming down with tremendous force. Zerach caught the sword between his hands, the blade inches from his face.

"I don't need a weapon to fuck you up. I'll just stomp your face in the ground."

He took the sword from Jaricus and smashed it into pieces. Now the battle has come down to bare knuckles. "Now that we're even, let's finish this," said Zerach with confidence.

"No matter, I'll still kill with or without my weapon. Plus, I'll enjoy torching you." Jaricus put up his fists. Zerach kicked him, but Jaricus grabbed his leg, slamming him to the ground. Zerach got back up; he punched Jaricus in the face. Zerach's swung missed. Jaricus lifted him up and body slammed him. "What's the matter, can't take it?"

Jaricus drove an elbow into Zerach's chest. "You're just a little bitch!" Jaricus threw him into a window in a building next to the one they were fighting on. Zerach stumbled to his feet. Jaricus headed straight for him, swooping down like a bird. Zerach jumped off a wall and pile drove Jaricus to the ground, smashing the flooring. They struggled with one another on the floor, tossing and tumbling. Jaricus kicked him off, sending Zerach into a wall. "You archangels never know when to quit even when you know you're beaten. But at least your kind is persistent," said Jaricus, wiping blood from his lip.

"I think it's the other way around, Jaricus. After all, it was your leader who blamed mankind for his failures. It was demons like you who followed him."

Alexa was still in the street with Tom and Jason. She sat at a bus stop while police, paramedics, firefighters, and rescue teams tried to evacuate all survivors in the downtown area. The place looked like a war zone. Everywhere, there was fire engulfing the building; the explosion from the police department caused the surrounding buildings to catch fire. It was like a terrorist attack had just been committed. Jason sat next to Alexa; he turned to her. "I want you to tell me honestly and truthfully. What the fuck is going on?"

Alexa looked at him. "I'm just as confused as you. I mean one day I'm just another girl and all of a sudden some guy is trying to kill me."

"Who's trying to kill you and why? Answer me!" exclaimed Jason.

"Look, I don't know. One minute I'm at a party and the next I have some guy trying to kill me!"

"It's all right, all right, listen, we need to get you out of here," said Jason, escorting Alexa off the bench. Tom ran up with a walkie-talkie in his hand. "Sir, we've located the fugitives; they're located at the thirty-second floor of the bank building straight ahead," said Tom.

"Okay, get her out of here. Send in the SWAT team in there. I don't want either one of those sons a bitches getting away."

Zerach and Jaricus, unaware of the SWAT team headed their way, kept fighting. Jason led the SWAT team up the building, slowly but swiftly making their way through.

"Set a formation, but swift and quiet," said Tom. Jaricus slammed Zerach to the floor. Tom could see them, just a few feet away. Jaricus had him pinned down.

"Can you hear it, Zerach? Can you hear the sound of the train coming to claim you?"

Jason was on his walkie-talkie. "All right, listen up! Make this clean and smooth. On my mark we go in there and apprehend them while they're still distracted. Copy."

Zerach saw the SWAT team creeping behind Jaricus, he smiled. "The real question is, can you hear the train coming for you?" said Zerach, kicking Jaricus off him then diving out of the way.

"FIRE!" yelled Tom. Jaricus was rattled with bullets, blood stained the walls; it was all over the floor and all over the ceiling. The SWAT team kept shooting, not stopping for anything. Jaricus was backed into a corner, being ripped apart by hot lead. Zerach slipped out of a window and out of the building. He landed on the sidewalk. People moved out of Zerach's way as he ran in search of Alexa. He was able to bypass all the other officers who were securing the scene. Zerach ran among the crowds of cops, news reporters, and bystanders. He searched for Alexa, trying to avoid attention to himself. Alexa was sitting in a squad car, shaking from being so nervous. She was worried about Zerach and looked around to see if she could see him anywhere. Zerach saw Alexa in a squad car. He ran to her and opened the driver's door.

"You okay?" asked Alexa.

"I'm fine, how about you?"

"I'm okay. Where's Jaricus?"

"He's busy with the cops. We need to get out of here." Zerach hit the gas and sped out of the scene undetected.

Chapter 7

"Hold your fire!" halted Tom. He walked over to see if Jaricus was dead. "He's gone."

"All right, let's get this mess cleaned up," said Jason, putting his gun back in his holster. Tom looked around. "Where's the other guy?"

"Shit! He's gone. I want all units to set up road blocks on every intersection and freeway entrance. He couldn't have gotten far."

Meanwhile, Jaricus moved his fingers, undetected. He balled his hand into a fist. He clenched it tight and said, "Nice try. That stung a little bit."

"What the fuck?" said one of the SWAT members. Jaricus rose up as if coming out of a coffin. His body rejuvenated again. "Now, my turn."

Jaricus grabbed a SWAT member by the face and tore his head off. The SWAT opened fire. Jaricus grabbed two of them, bashing their skulls together. The rest of the SWAT team, along with Tom and Jason, ran for their lives.

"There is no escape!" Jaricus punched through a SWAT member's mouth and then ripped another's jaw off. He picked up two machine guns, cornering some SWAT members against a window. Jaricus unloaded on them, their guts and blood laid on the floor and the walls. Jaricus kept shooting until they had all fallen out of the building.

A camera man caught the whole thing on tape as the dead SWAT members fell to their deaths. "The true god has arrived," Jaricus said to himself, laughing.

Jaricus kept his butchery, killing everyone and anyone in his way. Jaricus held a cop over his head and ripped him in half. The police fired back, but it was no use. Jaricus's body was like a machine; it kept going, never stopping. The SWAT team (what was left of them) ran out of the building. Tom, terrified behind belief, got on the radio. "I need back up! More back up! Oh shit!"

Heat came out of the walls of the building. Smoke filled the air, the windows melted. Flames took hold, the smoke blocking out the sun, plunging the city into darkness. Jaricus raised his hands. Then . . . the entire building exploded. Concrete fell to the ground, and dust filled air. People were coughing and running for their lives. Body parts fell from the sky like rain. Jaricus stood tall, proud, and arrogant. His red eyes could not be missed, for they could see through a person's heart; like an eagle can see its prey from far away. Jason stumbled to his feet. He could see Tom lying on the ground, face first.

Jason felt a presence like no other. He turned his head; the red sharp eyes of Jaricus stared at him. It was a stare of great power. Jason felt pure evil. Jaricus looked to the sky. "Where is your god? Where is your god! He is nowhere; he has abandoned all of you. What will you do? What will all of you do?" Jaricus turned into locusts; they swarmed the police, civilians, and anything else in their way. The insects had carried people into the air, devouring them.

"Shit! We have to get out of here!" Jason grabbed Tom. They took a police car and drove off. The locusts took off in a giant cluster, somewhat like a cloud. Jaricus, in the form of the locusts, continued his path of destruction as he flew into the night sky.

By this time, Zerach and Alexa were headed to their destination. Alexa was still shaken. She was more worried about Zerach than her own self. She thought to herself, wondering if she was falling in love with Zerach. Zerach was focused on getting Alexa to safety. "Are you okay?" he said, placing his hand on her knee. "I'm fine. Are you okay?" asked Alexa, putting her hand over his.

"I'm all right. Everything's going to be all right. All of this will be over soon. I promise."

"I trust you, Zerach," said Alexa, gripping Zerach's hand tighter.

He looked down at his hand. "I'll never let anything bad happen to you. I'll do whatever I have to do to protect you." Alexa never felt this way before. Neither did Zerach. Even he could not believe the feelings he had for Alexa.

Nothing was ever going to be the same for the two of them. Human and archangel forming a bond like no other. Zerach had Alexa on his mind; he held her tightly as they drove off. Alexa, looking over at Zerach, realized she was in love with him; she would never want to leave his side. They kept driving until they reached outside of the city limits. They were headed toward the countryside, where a church was present. There, Zerach was to meet with his fellow angels; one of them was Gabriel.

Zerach and Alexa were driving in the car. She had fallen asleep. Quietly, her head was resting against the seat. Her eyes shut, her arms were folded, shivering from the cold. Zerach noticed and turned the heater on. They got to a red light. Zerach looked over at her, and a hint of joy came over him. He rubbed Alexa's hair with his fingers gently. Zerach's fingers were soft and smooth. The light turned green, and Zerach continued on the route to the church. However, Jaricus was not far behind. He had perched himself in a tree. Now back in his original form, he smelled and tasted the air for any sign of Alexa.

Jaricus was still determined, still focused on his agenda. He was so close to achieving his goal he could taste it. Alexa's sent was stronger than before that he could taste it in the air. Like radar, Jaricus knew the direction they were traveling—north. Jaricus jumped from the tree and was on the move again, heading north.

Jason and Tom were in the squad car, still shaken by what happened. They were going to the hospital because Jason had been wounded. "You all right?" asked Tom, looking over at Jason. "I'll be fine, just a flesh wound." Jason kept his hand over his shoulder. "What the hell went on back there?" said Tom, his nerves causing him to tremble.

"I don't know," replied Jason, placing more tissue onto his wound. "It doesn't make sense; he was dead, I saw it. He just came back from the dead."

"That's crazy. The dead don't come back to life."

"Well, this guy did. You think he was in with the two suspects?"

"I doubt it; he tried to kill him," said Jason, adding more tissue. "All I know is, who or what he is, he's still on the loose."

"Shit! You think he was some sort of sick magician or something?" Jason looked at Tom with a stern look. "What I'm just saying . . . ," said Tom shrugging his shoulders.

They had pulled up to a hospital not far from downtown LA. Tom opened the door for Jason and escorted him inside. A nurse took them in; she was young, about twenty-one. She had black hair that came to her shoulders and eyes that were green. The uniform she wore was blue scrubs. On her feet were white tennis shoe and a name tag that said "Tasha."

"LAPD. My partner's been shot," said Tom, holding up his badge.

"Okay, sit him over there." Tasha went behind the desk and notified the doctor.

"You're going to be all right," said Tom, reassuring Jason.

"At least I can go on vacation," replied Jason. The doctor entered the room with some nurses. He was short and skinny. The doctor had on a white lab coat, with a brown tie underneath. His pants were black, and the shoes on his feet were brown. The doctor had a silver watch on his right hand. His wedding ring was on his left hand. The name badge on his coat read "Dr. Walter."

"Come on, get him in the emergency room. Quickly, quickly," Dr. Walter instructed his assistants. "What happened?"

"Had an incident in downtown Los Angeles. My partner was struck by a bullet."

Tasha handed the doctor some papers. "He has a gunshot wound to the left shoulder. It appears to be a flesh wound."

"All right, nothing like some stitches won't fix." The doctor put on some gloves, then headed into the room where Jason was waiting. Tom sat outside, rubbing his hands together, thinking about what happened. The entire event went over through his head several times. Tasha was behind the front desk; she looked over at Tom with a concerned look on her face. She peered over the desk at Tom. "You are going to be okay?"

"I'll be fine," Tom said looking up.

"Okay. I'm sure he'll be fine."

"Who?"

"Your partner. He'll be okay; you want something to drink?"

"Sure, I'll take a bottle of Jack," Tom said jokingly. Tasha smiled. "We don't serve alcohol here."

"Well, in that case I'll take a Coke." Tom smiled at her.

"One Coke coming right up." Tasha went to a vending machine and got a bottle of Coke. She handed it to Tom. He opened the bottle and took a few gulps. "That hit the spot. So how long you've been working here?"

"One year. But I've been a nurse for four years now."

"That's cool. What's it like?" asked Tom.

"It's really good, I get paid really well, plus benefits."

"That's nice," replied Tom.

"What's it like being a cop?" asked Tasha.

"Um . . . hectic. But it's a great career. I joined because I want to help people; you know, protect people from the bad guys."

"I see," replied Tasha, filing some paper work. Five minutes later, Jason came out with his arm in a sling. Dr. Walter escorted him out to the desk. "Now remember, take two a day, it'll help with the pain."

"Okay, Doctor, thanks a lot." Jason shook his hand.

"How's the arm?" asked Tom.

"It's fine; at least I get to take a vacation."

"Lucky," replied Tom. "You ready to get of here, sir?"

"Hell, yeah, I am."

Tom was escorting Jason outside. He turned around and went over to Tasha. "It was nice meeting you."

"You too."

"Listen, I was wondering if I could take you out sometime?" asked Tom.

"I don't know. I work a lot."

"C'mon, it'll be fun, I promise."

"Okay, here's my number." Tasha wrote her number on a sticky note and handed it to Tom.

"Will you come on! I'm tired and need to get home," said Jason, annoyed by Tom's childish behavior.

"I'll call you soon," said Tom, running back to Jason.

"You better call me!" said Tasha with a smile.

"What was all that about back there?"

"I just made a new friend that's all." Tom started up the car.

"Yeah sure . . . Just friends. I get shot and full of stitches and you're over here playing Mac daddy." Tom laughed as they pulled out of the parking lot.

After a long drive, Zerach and Alexa pulled into a church. It sat in the middle of the desert; it looked like a Spanish mansion. The church was large; on the front door was a black cross. The windows looked like gold from the outside; the roof was covered with red bricks that were laid perfectly. They were stacked in a beautiful pattern, like a row of flowers. The walls were white, like flower. The front steps were made of the same brick as the roof. Two angels, in human form, stood out from of the church. Just at the foot of the steps. One had red hair and was dressed like a member of the secret service. His name was Oliver. The second angel was armed with a rifle; he was dressed like a cowboy from the old West. His name is Donavan. Zerach walked in front of Alexa, approaching the angels. "I need to see Gabriel."

"He's inside, but first things first," said Oliver, stepping forth. Donavan stood back. "Come forward," Oliver said, pointing at Alexa. She looked at Zerach; he nodded his head. "Let me have a look at you." He reached his hands out. Alexa was hesitant, and Zerach pushed her forward. "Relax, I have to see something," said Oliver, placing his hands on her cheeks. Alexa felt awkward, not knowing what was going on. Oliver closed his eyes. For a few minutes, Alexa could suddenly see visions. Visions of herself being nailed at the cross; she began to yell in agony. "Be still, it's almost over," said Donavan. "What's happening to me!" yelled Alexa. She could feel the crown of thorns in her head and the nails piercing her flesh. Oliver held her cheeks, keeping still, not moving for a second.

"Relax, Alexa; it'll be over soon," said Zerach, trying to reassure Alexa that everything will be fine. Alexa still screamed in horror and pain. The visions got stronger; she's covered in a cloth, the same cloth they put over Jesus. Alexa suddenly blacked out. Her body went limp, and she could feel herself out of her body, as if ascending to another dimension. Alexa's body was on the floor. Oliver was still holding her cheeks; Zerach held her tight.

Alexa abruptly came back to consciousness. Oliver let go. He stood back and smiled. "Sorry for the scare, I just had to make sure."

"Make sure of what?"

"That you are the Holy Grail," said Donavan, walking up the doorsteps to the church. Zerach escorted Alexa in with Oliver behind them. They walked in quietly. Alexa looked around, and in front of her, at the altar, stood a man in a suit. It was Gabriel. He was wearing a brown suit, with a brown coat. His tie was red. His hair was black and slicked back, as if drenched with hair grease. Gabriel had on sunglasses that matched his outfit. He raised his hand. "Ah, finally, you showed up. I thought you were never going to make it." Gabriel turned to face Alexa and Zerach. He took off his glasses and walked down to Alexa. "Finally get to meet you. I've heard so much about you. You are very beautiful." Alexa stood there, trying to say something. "Why is Jaricus after me?"

"Yes that is a good question," said Gabriel, looking at Zerach. "You see, Alexa, you are so precious yet you have no idea how precious you are," Gabriel said, shifting his eyes to Alexa's.

"What does that mean?" asked Alexa, shaking.

"It means that you are the most valuable thing in this world. Because through you, men can become gods. Through you, peace can be brought to all who inhabit this world. In the hands of good, you're humanity's salvation. In the hands of evil, you are humanity's destruction."

Alexa felt a quiver come over her spine and into her head. Zerach placed his hands on her shoulders. "Are you okay?"

"I'm fine, just a little freaked out, that's all."

"Don't be. It's all meant to be," said Zerach, holding her.

"It's just, I didn't ask for this. I never asked to be a Holy Grail or a savior. I just want to live a normal life."

"It's fate. I—"

"It was destiny," Gabriel interrupted. He was sitting down, playing the piano. He was playing a beautiful song, never heard by human ears. "It was inevitable. You were chosen to be the savior or the destroyer."

"That's not fair. I don't want any part of this," said Alexa, afraid. "Life is never fair, and you are right. This was not your choice. It wasn't something you wanted, but it is something that was already decided way before you were born." Gabriel kept playing the song; as he did, lightning struck outside. The clouds turned grey and the sky roared like a lion. "The day came when Jesus was crucified. His last breath spelled the fate of what was to become. What was known as the Holy Grail." The song was so beautiful and powerful. It was like an ocean of melodies pounding the walls of the church. Zerach watched Gabriel. Like a spectator, he was intrigued by Gabriel's skills. Gabriel kept playing the song on the piano. "Alexa, you are the only one who can change the course of this world and possibly the next."

Alexa sighed she sat down in a seat and put her face in her hands. Zerach knelt down next to her. "I told you everything's going to be fine. I'm going to protect you."

"Zerach, I'm scared. What am I going to do?" replied Alexa, tears in her eyes. "There's no need to be afraid. You will be safe, no one is going to hurt you," said Zerach, running his hands through her hair. Alexa rested her head in his chest, holding Zerach tight. Gabriel stopped playing the piano. He got up and walked over to Zerach. "We need to talk."

"Okay, Alexa, I'll be right back." Zerach and Gabriel walked to the back of the church. In it was a small office with a chair and a desk. The walls were made of bricks and the ceiling was made of wood. There's a shelf with book stacked perfectly. Gabriel sat down, kicked his feet up on the desk and leaned back. Zerach sat down in front of him, crossing his leg.

"You know, he'll claim her as well," said Gabriel, slouching.

"I know he will. It'll be a matter when."

"He's waiting for you to kill Jaricus, then he'll make his move. Zerach, you're going to have to be sharper than ever. Don't think for a moment he won't send any of his . . . minions."

"I've thought about that already. I know he's buying his time. The important thing now is keeping Alexa safe from Jaricus." Gabriel got up and walked over to the book shelf. He pulled out a book with pages filled with angelic script. Gabriel walked over to Zerach, turning the pages. "You remember this one?"

"How could I forget." Gabriel sat the book down in front Zerach. The page upon which Gabriel turned to was a script that was written by Lucifer himself. "It seems only yesterday that he wrote these words. It's a shame what he became," said Zerach, holding the book.

"It sure is. He could've been a great angel, but like man, he became corrupted. You'd think after all these years he would've learned."

"Some don't. He'll never change, all he is, is just a power hungry, selfish angel who turned his back on his brethren." Gabriel sat back down. He looked at Zerach square in the eyes.

"Do you love her?" asked Gabriel.

"Alexa?"

"Of course Alexa, who else?" Zerach took a deep breath.

"What makes you think that?"

"Well, because I notice the way you look at her. I've noticed that you are very protective of her," said Gabriel, putting the book back. "Protecting her was assigned to me. It's my duty." replied Zerach, sitting on the desk. "Ah, yes, your duty. Perhaps your duty has turned into passion. All I know is she's in love with you."

"You've read her thoughts?"

"A little bit, and I must say they are quite powerful." Gabriel opened the door. He and Zerach walked out back to the main preaching area.

Alexa was sitting down with her feet on the seat. He sat down next to her. Donavan and Oliver kept watch outside. Everything seemed normal. No sign of a threat anywhere, just the cloudy sky and cold wind. Alexa shivered inside the church. Zerach took his coat off and put it on her to keep her warm.

Not too far away, Jaricus was en route to find Alexa. He could smell her miles away. He was in his human form now. Jaricus was on foot, walking down a deserted road surrounded by desert. He felt he'd travel like a human and decided to travel by car. All he needed to do was find one. Just over a hill, the shining lights of an automobile flashed ahead. Jaricus could hear the music playing from the car. He stood patiently on the side of the road, his eyes on his prize.

The car was a tour bus; it was brown with tinted windows. On the sides of the motor home were images of bikini models. The bus stopped, the door opened, and out came a young lady in a two piece. She had on high heels, her legs were long and smooth as silk. Her hair was brown; her green eyes were like gems. Jaricus licked his lips as he stared at her. Her hair blew in the wind, her sent was sweet roses. "Hey," she said softly with a bright smile. "Hey," Jaricus responded back, smirking. "You need a ride?" said the girl. Jaricus thought about it. He could easily kill this woman and anyone else on that bus. But why kill them when he can be driven to his destination. The plus side, he could have a lot of fun on the bus.

"Yeah, I need a ride." Jaricus followed the girl on to the bus. Jaricus got on the bus and, to his amazement, erotic beautiful women were aboard. They were all tall and beautiful. Some had on bikinis, others had on lingerie. A few of them were dressed as maids with tiny skirts so short, they exposed what was between their legs. Jaricus couldn't help but smile at the diversity of all the women he laid his eyes upon. Their odor was the scent of a thousand roses. Jaricus could hear their heartbeats, they sounded like a dozen drummer boys marching into battle.

All of the women had their eyes on Jaricus; it was as if they could sense some sort of evil about him that turned them all on. "Have a seat," said one of the girls. Jaricus sat down comfortably. Jaricus kicked back and relaxed, enjoying the show that these girls were putting on for him. To him, it was a break from all the stress. Jaricus figured he'd have some fun before he killed everyone on the bus. One of the women dressed as a French maid approached him. She was a redhead and had green eyes, with freckles on her cheeks. She knelt down next to Jaricus and whispered in his ear, "Where you from?" Jaricus looked up at her. He whispered back, "From hell." The girl laughed. "Wow, that's hot!" she said, laughing, holding her hand to her mouth. "Well, I'm from Los Angeles and the name's—"

"Carrie," said Jaricus, shaking her hand. "If you're wondering how I know your name, it's 'cause I heard your friend call you that."

"Oh really? For a moment I thought you were a stalker."

"No, I'm no stalker. I'm just a man trying to become more . . . elevated," said Jaricus.

"What do you mean by elevated?"

"What I mean is, I want to become more than what I am now. I want to achieve ultimate perfection. I want to become godlike," said Jaricus, scooting closer to Carrie.

Carrie was shocked and somewhat taken aback by Jaricus's comments. "Well, sounds like you have a lot of goals in mind."

"You have no idea."

Carrie leaned up against him, straddling Jaricus. "You look like you could use some company," said Carrie, her hands running through Jaricus's hair.

"So do you." Jaricus caressed her body with his fingers, taking off her outfit. The other girls stopped what they were doing and looked onward. Another girl walked up; she took off Jaricus's coat and kissed him on the neck. Carrie was moving down to Jaricus's pants, unbuckling his belt. A third girl dressed as a pirate joined in and kissed Jaricus's chest as he felt up the second girl that joined. A fourth girl with red hair and dressed like a fairy also joined the fun. Jaricus got every girl on the bus naked, and like a king, he made love to every one of them. Their bodies rubbing against each other created a heat that felt like fire. Jaricus took one after the other, making love to them. The sex was so intense that one can smell it in the air and steam was coming from the women's bodies, the whole bus felt like a steam room. The women moaned with incredible pleasure; Jaricus kept seducing the women one by one. The heat kept getting hotter and hotter; the women's eyes turned red like the color of blood. They were all engaging in fornication with great delight. Like true porn stars, these women performed with perfect eroticism, pleasing Jaricus as if he were a god, which was something Jaricus loved very much. Jaricus had cast a spell over the women, turning them into nymphomaniacs. Jaricus realized he could not have his fun for long, for he had business to tend to. "That's enough ladies." Jaricus snapped his fingers, and all women snapped out of it. "Wow, what happened?" asked one girl who just realized she was naked. "All I remember was blacking out and . . . why are we naked?" Asked another, putting a blanket over her body.

"It was fun while it lasted, but I really need to take care of some business. Now, if you don't mind, I'm going to need this bus." Jaricus opened the door to the bus and guided the women out of the door, who were all nude and confused.

Jaricus went up to the bus driver. "What the hell is going on?" said the driver.

"I'm sorry I must come, dear, this vehicle." Jaricus threw the driver out of the bus then sped off down the road ahead. Jaricus looked in the rearview mirror. He stopped the bus and stuck his hand out. He then snapped his fingers, and all the women, including the bus driver, burned to ashes. Their screams could be heard for miles. Jaricus got out and devoured their souls.

Jaricus looked to the skies; the clouds had turned black, and red lightning struck the ground. Jaricus laughed; he kept laughing as the weather became more violent. His thirst for destruction and death had become an addiction; Jaricus had become insane. Jaricus, still focused on what he came here to do, got back on the bus and drove toward his destination.

Alexa abruptly woke up from a deep sleep. Her body was sweaty; she was so wet it looked like she went for a swim in her clothes. Zerach was sitting at the edge of her bed, perched like a bird. "Zerach?"

"I'm here. You had another nightmare?" said Zerach, his back facing her. "It's Jaricus, I can feel him. He's coming for me; he's headed this way," said Alexa, terrified.

"I know he is, I could feel him too. He won't stop until you are dead."

"Am I going to die?" asked Alexa, shaking, tears coming down her face. Zerach turned to her and lay on top of her on the bed. "I promise I will never let that happen. I will protect you even if it means my life."

"But if you get killed? And—"

"That won't happen. No one is going to die except for Jaricus. Alexa, you will live on, I know it."

"How do you know?" said Alexa, lying down on the bed, putting her arms around Zerach who lay on top of her. "How do you know that I'm the Holy Grail?"

"I know because if you weren't, then God would not have sent me to protect you. I know because God made you so special; so special that no other person can ever come close to being as divine as you are." Alexa held Zerach close to her, and together they slept. Zerach's body was warm, and Alexa was no longer afraid. She felt safe with Zerach and grateful that God sent him to her. Alexa could sleep peacefully, knowing Zerach was there to watch over her, but it still didn't prevent the inevitable that was to come.

Jaricus was drawing near. The bus had a full tank of gas and a nice comfortable seat. Jaricus kept his foot on the gas and followed the scent of his prey to his destination. He knew that there were going to be obstacles in his way, but no matter, Jaricus was going to abolish them and claim his prize.

Miles back, Tom had taken Jason home and made sure he was okay. "Are you going to be all right?" asked Tom. "I'll be fine, just going to take some time off." Jason's wife walked in; her name was Carla. She had brown hair and green eyes and a cute little figure. She walked in with a glass of lemonade and some soup for Jason. "Thanks for looking out for him, Tom."

"No problem, Carla. I'll see you later, sir?"

"You bet your ass. And, Tom, watch yourself, okay? With this murdering son of a bitch on the loose, you never who's following you."

"I will. You get some rest, old man." Tom walked out and got into his car. Once he did, he got on his cell phone. He called Tasha, the girl he met at the hospital, to see if she wanted to get together. The phone rang, and a sweet voice of a woman answered, "Hello?" It was Tasha, and Tom was nervous at first but summoned the courage to say something. "Hello, may I speak to Tasha?"

"This is she," said Tasha in a sweet tone of voice. "Hi, this Tom, the guy you met at the hospital where I took my partner who got shot?"

Tasha hesitated for a moment, then finally remembered and answered back, "Oh yeah! I remember. What's up?"

"Nothing much, just wanted to know if you would like to go for dinner?"

"When?" replied Tasha. Tom stuttered for a moment, but the words finally came out. "How about tonight?" asked Tom, confident now that Tasha seemed interested. Tasha answered in an intrigued tone. "Tonight sounds good. What time?"

"We can meet somewhere if you like," said Tom, smiling and looking at himself in the mirror. "How about nine o'clock? We can go out for a movie." Tasha thought about it and agreed to meet up with Tom and see a movie. "Okay, that sounds good, as long as I pick what movie we see."

"That's fine by me. Where is the nearest theater from here?"

"There's one down at the fairgrounds, just west of where I work," said Tasha, excited about her date with Tom. "Okay, I can figure out where it is." Tom hung up the phone and cheered as he successfully managed to get a date with Tasha. He used his GPS to find out the nearest movie theater Tasha was talking about. He pulled up a map and programmed the computer to tell him how to get there. Tasha, on the other hand, was getting ready, nervous about her date. She had never dated a cop before, and she thought Tom was really attractive. A few minutes later, Tom arrived at the theater. He sat in a red car in front of the ticket booth, waiting for Tasha to arrive. As Tom was growing impatient, Tasha pulled up next to him. She was driving a Ford Fusion; it was dark blue, with shiny platinum rims. "Sorry I'm late; I got caught in traffic," said Tasha, giving Tom a hug.

"Its fine. I, uh . . . just got here myself." Tom was looking Tasha up and down 'cause she was really looking hot. Tasha was dressed in a black skirt that showed off her tone athletic legs, with black high heels to match. Her tank top was short and strapless that revealed her flat stomach. Tasha's belly button was pierced, along with both her ears; her hair was in a pony tail that stretched to her lower back. "You ready?" asked Tasha. Tom was startled, looking at Tasha's body. "Oh yeah, I'm ready. Do you know what movie you want to see? You were going to pick, remember?" said Tom, taking Tasha's hand. "I want to see *Red Wine*. I heard it was scary."

"Is that the movie where the guy finds out his neighbor is a vampire?"

"Yep. I've read the book, it was really good," said Tasha, looking up at Tom.

"All right, *Red Wine* it is."

They walked over to the ticket booth where the teller was sitting behind a desk in a chair. "Hello, how can I help you?" asked the teller, who was a young man about seventeen years old. "Two tickets for the ten o'clock *Red Wine*," said Tom.

"That would be twenty-one dollars and fifteen cents. Thank you and enjoy your show." Tom took the tickets and walked inside the theater with Tasha. "You want something to eat?"

"No, I'm fine. Let's eat after the show," said Tasha. Tom handed the tickets to the doorman, who showed them which theater hall to go to. Once Tom and Tasha found their seats, they sat down quietly watching the previews. In an attempt to put his arms around Tasha, Tom folded the arm rest up and put his arm over Tasha's shoulder. Instead of a rejection, Tasha laid across Tom in his lap as if they'd been together for years. Tom felt confident that something was going to happen between him and Tasha.

On the dirt, abandoned road leading to the church where Alexa and Zerach were, Jaricus was on his way in the bus he had taken to his destination. Jaricus could already sense that Zerach was not the only angel, but since he devoured more souls, Jaricus has become more powerful than before. Zerach could also feel the same thing. With each passing moment Jaricus drew near, at each moment, it seemed to Zerach that Jaricus's power was growing. He walked outside; he could feel Jaricus getting closer. Zerach closed his eyes; he could hear Jaricus's thoughts as if he were right next to him. The wind blew strong, knocking trees and plants over. He didn't budge. He stood as still as a statue waiting, wishing Jaricus would arrive. He hoped Jaricus would arrive soon just so he can kill him once and for all. Jaricus could also hear Zerach's thoughts. To him, they only made more eager to kill all of the angels, Alexa included.

Back at the movies, Tom was happily enjoying the date, as was Tasha. Their movie had ended, and they were now eating ice cream. "So how was work?" asked Tasha.

"Work was okay; my partner's doing fine."

"That's good. He looked a mess when he came in the emergency room," said Tasha, wiping chocolate ice cream from her cheek.

"He took a clean shot to the shoulder, but he'll be all right. How was work for you?"

"It was busy. A kid came in with a gunshot wound to the stomach. I'm not sure if he's going to make it," said Tasha, taking another bite of her ice cream.

"It's crazy out there. I've seen kids as young as nine who are already in gangs. When I look at them, I'd say they'll only live to be eighteen." Tom took a bite of his strawberry ice cream. He and Tasha kept walking; they walked around the plaza and headed for the fairgrounds.

Back at the church, Zerach and the angels were preparing themselves for a showdown between Jaricus. Gabriel walked outside to check on Zerach. "He's coming near, I can feel him," Gabriel said. "I can feel him, too, and the souls that have become a part of him." Gabriel sat down on a step. Zerach was standing, his fists clenched. "Relax, don't let him get to you. His time will come," said Gabriel, playing a saxophone. "I'm trying to focus," replied Zerach, standing still. "Don't focus too much or you'll lose sight of your objective. He'll use your emotions to his advantage." Jaricus was getting closer; he could feel Zerach and the other angels' energy. However, it was Zerach's energy he felt the most, and it only made him more eager to kill him. It made Jaricus so eager that he could do nothing but smile. "Almost there. Time of the angels on this earth will soon be at an end," Jaricus said to himself, going even faster. Zerach jumped on the roof of the church. He focused his energy on what may come. Zerach already knows what to expect from Jaricus, but he didn't know what the outcome may be. Tom was walking Tasha to her car, they're holding hands. The night is cold and the moon is full. As Tom takes her to her car Tasha kisses him on the lips. "I had a great time tonight," said Tasha, getting in her car. "Me too, I'll uh . . . see you soon?"

"Sure," replied Tasha, pulling out of her parking space.

"Okay." Tom got in his car with a smile on his face. He started the engine then drove off, heading home.

Back at the church, Alexa was sitting on the bed where she had slept. She got up, put on a shirt and sweat pants, and then walked outside. She saw Zerach standing on the roof, staring at the horizon. "What are you doing up there?" asked Alexa curiously. Zerach looked down and then turned away. "You shouldn't be out here. It's too dangerous," he said, still staring at the horizon. "What do you mean? There's nothing out here," said Alexa, looking up at Zerach. "Jaricus will be here soon; the first he'll do is find you and kill you. I won't let that happen." He jumped down to

Alexa, putting is hands on her waist. "Please go inside. I can't risk anything happening to you."

"But I want to be with you," said Alexa, placing her hands on Zerach's cheeks. He grabbed her hands and kissed them and looked at her real deep into her eyes as if gazing into a maze. "I can't defend you from Jaricus if I'm worrying about you. I need to stay focused, so when he arrives, promise me you'll stay inside. You're safer in the church, trust me. Since Jaricus is a demon, he cannot step foot inside a church."

Alexa put her arms around him, putting her face into his chest. "I don't know what I'd do if I lost you. I can't bear the thought of it."

"Don't worry about me," said Zerach with a smile. "You won't have to; after all, I'm an angel." Zerach kissed Alexa on the lips, who in return kissed him back. "Go inside and please stay there." Alexa walked back into the church and sat down in a seat. She curled her legs as if she were cold when, in fact, she worried about Zerach.

Jaricus was in the bus coming closer and closer. He could see the church where Zerach, Gabriel, Donavan, Oliver, and Alexa were hiding out. "There it is!" said Jaricus. Zerach stopped in his tracks; he looked up at Gabriel. "He's here." Donavan and Oliver stood behind Zerach, and Gabriel stood in front of Zerach. Jaricus stepped on the gas pedal even harder. This time, he could see the four archangels. Like a missile, Jaricus aimed right for them, attempting to crush them with the bus. Oliver stepped in front of Zerach and pressed his head right into the bus. Since

Oliver was an archangel, his body was like a titanium wall. Jaricus flew out of the bus head first then barrel-rolled onto the ground and slamming into a tree. The tree instantly split in half like a small branch. The bus was completely totaled; its front end looked like a smashed tomato. The back end looked like a crushed soda can, and Jaricus was bleeding from his head. His was twisted to the side, and, with a look of surprise, he put his head back in place. The wound on his head healed instantly. He stood up with eyes fixed on Zerach. "That was clever move, but too bad it won't happen again."

"Jaricus, I suggest you go back to hell. You don't stand a chance," said Gabriel, stepping forth.

"Ah, Gabriel, the angel of death. It's been so long since we've last talked."

"Your day on this earth is over, Jaricus. The girl belongs to the Lord. Leave."

Chapter 8

Jaricus's body began to heat up as his power began to grow. Steam was coming from him like a teapot, and his eyes were red. "If that's the best you can do, then I'm very disappointed. Perhaps you realize you can't stop me." Zerach was wielding his sword; Gabriel pulled out a stick that extended into a double-headed spear. Donavan pulled out his rifle and cocked back the hammer. Oliver put on some black gloves and then pulled out a whip that was made from a long chain. The chain had a large blade at the end of it that was shaped like a hook. Jaricus just smiled at the fact that all the archangels would pull out such weapons. "I had enough of this!" said Donavan, firing the gun. The bullet was no ordinary bullet. It hit its target no matter how fast or where the target was. Donavan was able to command the bullet were to find its target and where to hit it. Donavan fired his weapon. Jaricus leaped into the air, and the bullet followed him like a guided missile. Jaricus was struck by the bullet, yet he still hit the ground standing. Donavan fired again. This time, Jaricus didn't attempt to move out of the way; instead, he stood, still laughing.

"What the fuck?" said Donavan. Jaricus started laughing; his body was consumed with a red energy field around him. "He's gotten stronger," Zerach said, clenching his sword, ready for any attack from Jaricus.

"Is that all you possess?"

"We possess enough to kill you," said Gabriel.

"In that case, come on with it." All four angels attacked. Jaricus wielded two swords and blocked whatever attack they used against him. Oliver, wielding his chain whip, lashed the blade at Jaricus. Jaricus grabbed the chain and slammed Oliver to the ground; then Zerach came forth with his blade. Jaricus blocked the sword, knocking it out of his hands. Jaricus then kicked Zerach to the ground. Gabriel stepped up to challenge Jaricus. With his spear, Gabriel managed to stab Jaricus in the shoulder and flung him in the air. Zerach leaped after him. Jaricus blasted him in the face with demon energy. Zerach fell to the ground with tremendous impact. Out of nowhere, Gabriel and Donavan came after Jaricus. They double-teamed him, trying to knock him out of the sky. Donavan fired another round but missed, and Jaricus stabbed him in the chest with his swords. Gabriel managed to punch Jaricus in the face, thus freeing Donavan from the blades. Jaricus dropped his swords, and Gabriel stabbed him in the ribs, slamming Jaricus to the ground. The impact created an explosion that nearly decimated the church. "You're not strong enough, Jaricus. You're better off dying."

"What you don't understand, Gabriel, is," Jaricus said, while struggling to pry the spear from his rib, "that I will succeed and that your god will be no more." Jaricus pulled the spear out of his ribs. Gabriel was thrown in the air, and Jaricus threw the spear, aiming for Gabriel. The spear struck Gabriel in the stomach, and he landed in a tree, stuck to the trunk.

"Gabriel!" yelled Zerach, rushing to his aid.

"Don't worry about me, I'll be fine. Just finish him off."

Zerach turned to face Jaricus, who was overcome with hate. "C'mon, angels, you self-proclaimed soldiers of God."

Zerach pulled his sword apart by the handle, and it split into two. He then put them together to create a double-bladed sword. "Oliver, Donavan, Gabriel, get in the church and look out for Alexa."

"What are you thinking?" said Oliver.

"Leave him be. This isn't our fight; he and Jaricus have unfinished business," Gabriel said.

"Jaricus, mark this as the last day of the rest your life!" Zerach told Jaricus, setting himself for a fight.

"Oh, my dear Zerach, I think not, for today marks the end of this world, for it will be mine."

Zerach charged toward Jaricus with great speed. Jaricus moved out of the way, blocking Zerach's attack. Jaricus swung his sword, aiming for Zerach's head. He blocked the blade and managed to cut off Jaricus's arm. "Ah! Bastard!" Jaricus yelled, still fighting with only one arm. Jaricus once again jumped into the air with Zerach close behind him. Inside the church, Alexa was on her knees, praying for Zerach's safety. "Please, God, watch over Zerach. You sent him to protect me, please protect him." Gabriel came from behind her, placing his hands on her shoulders. "He'll be fine. You have nothing to worry about."

"But why won't you help him?" asked Alexa, tears coming to her eyes.

"Because God chose him to protect the Holy Grail. So this is his fight."

Zerach and Jaricus continued their battle. This time, they were back on the ground. Jaricus only had one arm, but he was still determined to kill him. "You had enough?" said Zerach. Jaricus replied with a smile, "I'm just getting warmed up." Jaricus and Zerach continued their fight; their clash loud and intense, fighting to the death. Zerach managed to cut off Jaricus's other arm.

"Don't be in such a rush." Jaricus instantly grew back both of his arms. "What's wrong? Not as easy as you thought?"

"No, I was just getting a feel for my swords," said Zerach as he and Jaricus struck each other again, their blades striking each other so ferociously that sparks flew, lighting the ground ablaze. The fire made a circle around them, like a ring of death, yet neither one of them budged. They both stood their ground firmly and stared each other down, waiting to see who would make the first move. "Zerach, this fire represents what is left of your life on this earth. Surely it will burn out, and I will be the water that puts it out."

"Perhaps, Jaricus, this fire represents what's left of your time on this earth. It will be put out and I am the water that destroys it." Zerach detached his double-headed sword. Jaricus, only having one sword, knew he did not have the advantage. He kicked Zerach in the chest, nearly causing him to land in the fire. Jaricus punched the ground, causing the ground to split. Zerach flipped in the air, landing on the roof of the church. Jaricus was above him in just seconds and coming with his sword ready to cut him in half. But there was a problem. As Jaricus came just an inch of Zerach's face, he was frozen. The reason is because he is a demon and cannot enter a church.

"I guess this is going to be easier than I thought," said Zerach, sticking both blades in Jaricus's ribs and then plummeting him to the ground and sticking him to a tree.

"Fuck!"

"Have a nice trip to hell!" Zerach pulled the swords from Jaricus and cut his head off. The blood sprayed like a fountain. Jaricus's body went limp, and his head rolled next to Zerach's feet. He put his swords away in his coat. He then picked up Jaricus's head and, with the use of a small knife, stuck it to a large cross that was outside the church. Alexa embraced him the moment she saw him. Gabriel stepped forth with his arms opened. "It isn't done."

Alexa turned to him with worry. "Wait, it's not over?"

"No, it isn't. That's why you and I have to leave now," said Zerach, holding Alexa.

"But Jaricus is gone. I saw you kill him."

"Alexa, you have to understand that there are many ways Jaricus can come back," said Gabriel, looking at Zerach. "Let's go; we have to move quick." Zerach gave Alexa his coat to keep her warm. "Well, with that being said, there is just one more thing we have to do before we part." Oliver took out some gasoline and wet the floor down. Once he was finished, Donavan lit a match, and a fire was started. Zerach quickly went outside and got Jaricus's head along with his body. He placed them on the altar so the body could burn with the church. They all went outside and watched as the church burned down to the ground. This was an attempt to destroy any evidence of the archangels ever being there and to buy time for Zerach to get Alexa to another safe location. "This is it. This is your chance to find safety somewhere else and hope this may keep Jaricus dead," said Gabriel, hugging Zerach. "Thank you for everything," said Alexa, also giving Gabriel a hug.

"Well, I guess this is farewell. Hopefully, the next time I see you, it won't be in a time of war."

Zerach and Alexa got back into their car. Oliver approached, still holding his gun and whispered in Zerach's ear, "Take care."

Zerach turned the car on and drove off down the road, heading west, getting as far away as possible. Alexa looked out of the window; she had a question on her mind. "Zerach, will it be soon that I'll be safe?"

"No. I'm afraid not. There are still others who want to kill you."

Alexa sighed. She looked at Zerach and placed her hand on his lap. "Well, let's not think about that. How about we just enjoy the trip?" said Alexa. Zerach couldn't help but smile. "Sounds good to me."

They drove off until they could not be seen. Back at his house, Tom got a phone call from an officer. The call was about a fire that had burned a church. "What are you talking about? A church burned down? When? Shit! I'm on my way." Tom hung up his phone, grabbed his jacket, and headed to the location where the church had burned. He arrived to see firefighters putting out the remainder of the fire as well as police officers who created a perimeter around the site. "LAPD," said Tom, flashing his badge. "How'd the fire start?"

"Someone wet the place down with gasoline and then lit a match," said a firefighter, holding what was left of a pack of matches. Tom got a phone call from his boss over at his headquarters. "Sir, with all due respect, why was I called over here? This is out of my jurisdiction." On the other line, Tom's boss pointed out that the fire was linked to the case of the massacre that had taken place a few days earlier. Tom entered the burned site. The church was completely torched, and there was nothing left but ruble. On the ground was a familiar picture imprinted on the church floor. It was the same cross image that Tom had seen with Jason at the crime scene of the massacre. Tom immediately pulled out his camera and took several pictures of the image. Tom couldn't believe his eyes. He called Jason to inform him about the news. "Jason, it's me Tom."

"What is it?" replied Jason, still groggy from some medicine he took. "I'm here at this church in the middle of the desert."

"What are you doing there?" asked Jason, coughing.

"A church was burned down, and you better come and see what I found."

"What did you find?"

"On the floor, engraved was that cross we found at that massacre. Sir, I think you should take a look at it."

"Damn! All right, meet me at my house tomorrow morning," said Jason. He hung up the phone and lay back in his bed. Carla walked in with some water, setting down next to Jason. "Is everything okay?"

"Yeah, honey, everything is fine."

Chapter 9

Tom was at home, sitting at his desk, studying the pictures he took at the burned site of the church. Tom was online searching for the image of the cross, hoping there may be some meaning behind it. Tom was unsuccessful in his research and shut down the computer. Stricken with exhaustion, Tom changed into his pajamas and went to sleep.

The following morning, a knock was at Tom's door. Feeling groggy and tired, he slowly went to the door. He peered out of the window and saw Jason standing at his doorstep, with his arm in a sling. His black suit was wet with water 'cause it had been raining outside. "Hey, what's going on?" asked Tom.

"Said you had some pictures to show me?" replied Jason, walking inside. "Yeah, hold on, let me get dressed." Tom went into his bedroom and put on some jeans and a white T-shirt. "Here it is." Tom handed Jason the pictures, then heads in the kitchen to make some coffee.

"These were taken from the site?"

"Yep, it's exactly like the cross we found at the house where that massacre took place."

Jason could not believe what he was seeing. "Yep, that's definitely it. I think I can ask a friend of mine what it is. He might know."

"Who's your friend?" asked Tom. "He's an archeologist. He's an expert in ancient artifacts. If anyone knows what this is, he's the one."

Tom gave Jason a cup of coffee and then sat down on his couch. "Where do we go from here, sir?" asked Tom. Jason stood up, putting his hands in his pockets.

"We pick up where we left off." Jason took his cup of coffee and walked out of the house to his car. Tom sat back, thinking to himself of the mystery surrounding the cross.

Zerach and Alexa were miles away. They had stopped at a hotel for the night, feeling exhausted. Alexa threw herself on the bed as Zerach sat next to her, comforting her as best he could. "Is it over?" asked Alexa, resting her eyes.

"It is for now. You should get some rest. We have to leave in the morning." Alexa looked up at Zerach. "Can you sleep with me tonight? I feel safe when I'm in your arms." Zerach took off his coat and crawled into bed with Alexa, putting his arms around her to keep her warm and safe. They slept peacefully and kept each other warm until Zerach sat up due to a peculiar noise. He got up, walked outside to the balcony, and saw Lucifer sitting in a chair on the balcony. He was dressed in a blue suit with a black cane in his hands. "Hello, Zerach. It's been a long time."

"You can't have her. If you lay a hand on her, I'll kill you."

"Relax, I didn't come here to fight," said Lucifer, leaning back in his seat. "I just came here to talk. That's all."

"Talk about what?"

"You, of course. I want to talk about you and what I can offer you."

"Forget it, I'm not in the mood. You should leave now."

"Don't be so antsy, brother. I am just here to give you an offer. An ultimatum, that's all."

Zerach knew better than to trust him. He knew that Lucifer had some sort of trick up his sleeve. "What is it you want?" Zerach asked, stepping back, keeping a close eye on Lucifer. "This fight over this girl is useless. I mean, what do you have to gain from all of this? It's not like you're being rewarded for protecting her."

"It's not about being rewarded; it's about doing as you are told."

"Doing as you're told, huh? I'm not surprised you were always so eager to make him proud. Always so desperate to be his favorite. How pathetic," said Lucifer, spitting on the ground.

"Well, unlike some, I am willing to put others before myself and not use deceit to tempt or to destroy others. Do you really think I am that stupid? To fall for your tricks? I have my will and my faith, and I will do what needs to be done to ensure the safety of this young woman. I will see to it that you will not succeed in whatever your mission may be. And I will stop you at all costs," said Zerach, raising his finger at Lucifer.

"You're such a fool. Here I am trying to make a truce, trying to reason with you and you go spit it back in my fucking face! This isn't over, Zerachiel," said Lucifer. He jumped off the balcony, disappearing out of sight.

"Like hell it's over, it's just begun." Zerach went back inside the room and sat on the bed, looking at Alexa, fast asleep. "It's far from over."

After leaving the burned scene, Tom and Jason were back on their way to nearby station in Los Angeles to analyze any evidence that was collected. "You think we got anything so far?" asked Tom, sitting in the driver's seat. "I don't know. That place was in pretty bad shape. We can just hope there was something left behind there or we have to start from scratch." They pulled into the station, in the rear entry. They got out and enter the back door. At the back of the building, it read, "Los Angeles Police Department." Once they entered the building, Tom and Jason went to the front desk, where a heavyweight officer was filing some papers. The desk was shielded by a black cage, and only a small slot to pass things through. "How can I help you, gentlemen?" asked the officer, approaching the counter. Tom and Jason held their badges. "We're to see some evidence that might've just come in," said Jason.

"Okay, down that hall, gentlemen."

Tom and Jason walked down a narrow hall, which led to the evidence room. Jason held in his hands a piece of paper with writing on it, detailing where the evidence was filed. They searched up and down each shelf and file cabinet. "Here it is." Tom reached up and grabbed a small plastic bottle. In it was red ash, which was odd, considering he had never seen anything like it before. "What the hell is this?" asked Tom, showing the container to Jason. "I don't know, looks like ash."

"That's all they got? Ash?"

"Take a good look at it, what do you notice?"

"It's red," replied Tom, looking confused.

"Exactly, have you ever seen red ash before?" asked Jason, taking the container out of Tom's hand. "We gotta get this analyzed and see where it came from. Looks like we have something here," said Jason, walking out of the evidence room.

"Well, what do you think it could be? Some remains from the church itself," Tom said, following Jason. "I know a guy who can get this tested and see what it may be."

"What's this friend's name?" asked Tom, getting into the driver's side.

"Dr. Wilkoff. He and I go way back. He did some work for me back in the day. He now has his own private forensics firm," said Jason, putting the container in his pocket.

"Where's this guy at?"

"Just down the road here, on Long Beach Boulevard." Tom made his way toward Long Beach. They finally came up to a clinic, which was a house. It belonged to Dr. Wilkoff, a Russian who came to the United States as a teenager. He was a good friend of Jason and helped solve many of Jason's cases. Tom and Jason approached the front door and rang the doorbell. "Who is it?" said Dr. Wilkoff in a Russian accent.

"It's me, Jason. Open up." The door opened and there was Dr. Wilkoff, a short chubby man with glasses and a black beard. His hair was beginning to turn grey, so he often wore a hat. He had on brown slippers and red sweat pants and had on a white T-shirt, which was covered by a brown robe.

"Jason, my man, how good to see you! How've you been? Please come in."

"I've been good. This is my partner Tom. Tom, this is Dr. Wilkoff."

"Nice to meet you," said Tom, shaking Dr. Wilkoff's hand. "It's a pleasure, so what brings you boys here? Beer?"

"No thanks, we came by to see if you can help us out."

"Okay."

"Here, take a look at this." Jason handed Dr. Wilkoff the plastic container with the red ash inside. "This is unusual, where did you find it?"

"It's evidence collected from a fire that burned down a church. It was found on the floor." Dr. Wilkoff took a closer look at it, puzzled on what it could be. "Well, it's definitely some sort of powder. I'll have to run some tests."

"How long would it take?" asked Tom.

"Not long. Come, you can see for yourselves." Tom and Jason followed him to his lab out back. It wasn't too big, but big enough to analyze evidence taken from crime scenes. There was a small table on it was a microscope and some trays containing DNA evidence. Under the table were chemicals sealed shut that read toxic. "Let me have a closer look at it; hopefully, I can come up with a general idea of what it may be." Dr. Wilkoff took a small sample of the red ash and placed it under his microscope. "This is interesting," he said, perking up.

"What is it?" asked Jason, leaning over his shoulder. "I have never seen anything like this before. It appears it's something that doesn't exist at least in our world," replied Dr. Wilkoff. "It doesn't seem to belong to any person or thing. It may have come from something that has yet to be discovered." Tom looked at Jason with shocked eyes, neither knew what to think or do.

"All right. Well, thanks for everything; you've been a good help."

"I'm here if you need anything. You boys take care now." Dr. Wilkoff shook Jason and Tom's hands before walking them out to their car.

"Damn! That's some weird shit," said Tom, scratching his head. Jason looked at the ash inside the container, "This case is getting weirder and weirder." They turned on the car and took off, heading back to the freeway. The plastic cup containing the red ash rested in the glove compartment, swaying back and forth as the car moved.

Alexa was brushing up in the restroom of the hotel. She was a bit shaken about the past few days but was getting used to the idea of being mankind's fate. "So what exactly is my purpose as this holy grail?" asked Alexa, walking into the living-room area. Zerach was sitting at a desk, looking on the computer. "To be exact, your purpose is the fate of mankind."

"I meant, tell me from the beginning the whole story. Plot, setting, facts, tell me how this all began." Zerach turned to Alexa, his eyes fixed on hers. He sat back in his seat, crossing his legs, preparing himself to tell Alexa what she wanted to know. "Well, your purpose is to be the most divine entity God has ever created. For you are the being which will determine the fate of this world in the hands of good or evil."

"What do you mean?" asked Alexa, sitting on the bed. "What I mean is you are the key to humanity's existence, whether being in God's hands or Jaricus's hands. That is why the Lord sent me to protect you, to ensure that you remain in the hands of good." Alexa stood in front of Zerach to get his attention. "What if Jaricus gets me?"

Zerach looked up at Alexa. "If Jaricus gets his hands on you then . . . mankind is doomed." Alexa sat back on the bed, confused to what Zerach just told her. "I'm sorry, but I'm confused."

"What I am saying is in the hands of good, you're humanity's salvation, but in the hands of evil, you're humanity's destruction. My reason for being on this earth is to ensure that you don't fall into the hands of evil."

"Who said that I was the fine line that dictated the fate of the world?" Alexa exclaimed, pounding her fists into the bed. Zerach got up and grabbed her arms, then held her close to him. "Relax, nothing bad is going to happen to you. You have my word. I will protect you, no matter what, no matter what it takes." Alexa began to cry. She rested her head against Zerach's chest. He put his arms around her to comfort her; she too held him close to herself. "I just want a normal life, I didn't ask for any of this!" She sobbed, clenching Zerach's coat. "Sometimes, we don't always get what we want, but we all have a purpose in life. We just have to find that purpose and use what has been granted to us in order to make a difference." Zerach held her close to him.

Chapter 10

Tom and Jason were on their way to Denny's. They pulled up in the parking lot next to a trailer. It was ten o'clock at night, and the clouds were coming in from the west. Thunder was heard overhead, accompanied by lightning. "Damn forecast didn't mention anything about a storm," said Tom, walking up the steps to Denny's. "Well, sometimes we think we can control things, only to find out we can't," replied Jason. They entered Denny's and were greeted by a young man who looked to be in his twenties, "Hello and welcome to Denny's. Sit wherever you like."

Jason and Tom took a seat by a window. Lightning intensified as flashes of white light lit up the sky. "Shit! It's pretty intense, said Tom, looking out the window. Jason was busy looking at the menu when the waitress walked up. "You boys ready to order?"

"I know what I want," said Tom, looking right up at the waitress who was a young redhead, whose hair came down her shoulders. She also had sparkling blue eyes and broad hips and legs that can make a man melt. "I would like a hamburger and some fries with a vanilla cake," said Jason.

"I'll have the same thing," said Tom, his mouth halfway open, drooling over the waitress.

"Okie-dokie, coming right up."

Jason nudged Tom aggressively and then laughed. "What, what is it?"

"C'mon, you idiot, can you make it any obvious?" said Jason, slouching in his seat. "What, I was watching the television."

"Right, hotshot, I saw those eyes. You were looking right at her tits."

"I was .... whatever. Anyways, what the hell are we going to do about this case? We've been on it for weeks now and don't have a damn thing," said Tom, putting the menu aside. "Well, let's take a look at what we've got so far. First was the massacre, from there we got a name, some girl named Alexa."

"Oh, and don't forget that nut job boyfriend of hers. As well as that homicidal maniac who they claimed to be after them." The waitress came back with their meals and set them on the table. Jason took a sip of his soda and then took a bite out of his burger. "So what's next?" asked Tom, stuffing fries into his mouth. "We pick up where we left off . . . we get that dust analyzed and see whether or not it belonged to the arsonist."

"This whole thing is getting weirder and weirder. You think that guy and that chick were responsible for that massacre and the fire? 'Cause ever since we interrogated them, all this crazy shit keeps happening," said Tom, taking another bite of his burger. "That's an interesting point. If they themselves didn't commit the crimes, they didn't definitely know who did.

She was certain the guy who shot me was after them. Don't forget, we also have eye witnesses to the massacre who claimed they saw Alexa leave with the guy interrogated. Zerach was his name, right?"

"Yeah." Jason slouched in his seat. "We need to find those two fast and bring them into custody. Plus that guy who killed our men." Tom interrupted. "No shit, that guy took thousands of rounds and just got back up like it was nothing. Shit, like I said before, this case is getting weirder by the days." The two agents ate their food, not realizing the dust they had collected, which was sitting in the glove compartment, was coming to life. The cap of the bottle popped open, and the dust started to spill out. The clump of dust got bigger and bigger until it was able to prop open the glove compartment. The dust spilled out onto the floor of the car, and like water, it started to overflow. The windows shattered and the car was being tilted on its side. The tires popped and went flat, the back of the car bent back as the front of the car was slanted upward. The dust poured out of the car like an overflowing bucket. Tom and Jason were still inside Denny's and didn't notice what was happening outside. The dust collected on the pavement; like a giant mound of ash, it swirled like a tornado taking form. The waitress was sitting at a table, counting her tips, when she caught the glimpse of the dust swirling around outside. "What the hell is that?" The manager got up and walked over to the window. "What in the world?" Tom and Jason got up, they ran to the front door. They were both speechless, looking on as the cloud of dust began to take shape. First, the arms has formed, then the legs, the torso, and finally the head. When the dust faded away, there stood Jaricus in perfect form. He looked brand new, not flaws on him whatsoever; it was as if he were a phoenix that rose from the ashes. Unsaved, just like an antique car in mint condition; his eyes, cherry red, looked right through Tom and Jason. "Shit, it's him! It's him!" Tom yelled, drawing his gun. He and Jason fired their guns, causing no damage to Jaricus. "Yes, it's me." Black steam evaporated from his skin, engulfing him in a black cloud that reeked of burned smoke. "Everyone, get inside!" yelled Jason. One customer didn't listen and tried to run away. But Jaricus released a clump of substance, which seemed to be tar, from his chest and covered the man with it. Once Jaricus had him captured, he took him into his body. "Now I've got your soul. Fuck it! I'll take all of you with me!" Jaricus unleashed a legion of familiars, which were demonic souls that poured into Denny's restaurant, consuming all in sight. Tom and Jason moved out of the way as the people were robbed of their souls. These souls, once put inside Jaricus, made him stronger than before. Tom and Jason shot and ran at the same time. They hid in an alleyway; they could hear Jaricus approaching. "Shit! Did you see that? Where the fuck did he come from?" exclaimed Tom, reloading his weapon. "Shut up! I hear him," said Jason, getting for what was coming. Jaricus turned the corner. "I see you, he-he-he-he! Your weapons are useless against me. But I need to know something. I was wondering if you knew where someone is. Don't worry, your visions will tell me." Jaricus grabbed Tom and slammed him against the wall. "Put him down!" yelled Jason. Jaricus smacked him across the face, sending him into a trash can. "Now, let's see what you can show me." Jaricus held Tom by the head. He looked deep into Tom's eyes. He saw all of Tom's memories from the time he was a little boy to the present. Jaricus also saw Alexa when she was being interrogated by Tom. Jaricus saw Zerach and Alexa escape and then the memories faded. "Dammit, guess I got to start from scratch." Jaricus dropped Tom. Jaricus looked to the sky, as trying to find some sort of answer to his problem. The wind began to blow rapidly, and storm clouds rolled in. The thunder roared, sounding like a bomb. Red lightning lit up the black sky, striking the earth with smoldering heat. Jaricus opened his wings and, with a gust of energy, took off into the sky. Jason was dazed, and Tom was coughing, trying to get back on his feet. "Jason, c'mon, we got to get out of here." Jason stood up, dazed and shaken. "C'mon, partner, we need to get to the car quick," said Tom, grabbing Jason and guiding him to the car. "What the hell was that?"

"Shit! How should I know? He literally looked right through me as if he could see in me," said Tom, realizing the car was trashed. "Dammit! The hell are we going to do now?"

"That was impossible; there's no way he could've . . . read my whole life," said Tom in disbelief. "I get the feeling he's looking for someone. It was the girl Alexa. He was looking for her," said Tom, leaning against the wall next to Jason. Zerach and Alexa were at the hotel; it was midnight. The area was calm and quiet, peaceful. Alexa was fast asleep with Zerach by her side. Suddenly, Zerach sprang up as if waking up from a nightmare. "We have to go. Get up!"

"What's the matter?"

"Jaricus, he's come back, and he'll eventually be on his way here. We have to leave as soon as possible." Alexa got up without hesitation. She put on her clothes, and she and Zerach headed out of the hotel. "How do you know he's coming?" asked Alexa frantically.

"I felt his presence. He's been resurrected, and he'll track you down."

"But how did he get resurrected? Zerach, stop!" Zerach and Alexa stopped in their tracks. "Listen, let's calm down for a minute, okay? Look, he was burned in the fire. I highly doubt he came back from that."

"You have no idea what you're talking about. He's alive, and he is coming for you. Now hurry up and go." Zerach grabbed Alexa by the arm, dragging her to an abandoned truck. They got inside the truck and sped out of the parking structure onto the moonlit road.